MW00881061

THE
UNBEATABLE
LILY HONG

DIANA MA

THE UNBEATABLE LILY HONG

CLARION BOOKS
An Imprint of HarperCollins*Publishers*

To Liam and Kieran—
my creative, strong-willed children
who inspired me to write this story

ONE

THE TENSION THICKENS AS I eye Max Zhang across the aisle in our seventh-grade Honors English class. Max tries to stare me down, but I refuse to blink, budge, or do anything to make him think he's going to win. *Nope, I will not be intimidated.* Pulling myself up to my full height of four feet, eleven inches (which, believe it or not, is freakishly tall for a twelve-year-old Chinese girl), I shoot imaginary lasers of doom from my eyes at him.

Max then pulls himself up to *his* full height of four feet, ten point five inches (because no way is he as tall as I am), and full-on smirks at me. Our English teacher, Mr. Orwell, tells us the verb *smirk* is overused, but can I help it if there's no better way to describe how Max curls up the corner of his lips like he's Count Dracula mocking his victims?

In my corner of the ring (okay, on my side of the aisle),

there's Lauren and Kelli. They're sitting on either side of me, and I imagine Lauren spraying me down with water and Kelli popping a mouthguard into my mouth as I go round one thousand and one with Max.

In reality, Lauren is drafting another email to our principal about the need for compostable utensils in the cafeteria, tucking her black braids behind her ear as she scribbles in her notebook. And Kelli is twirling her long red hair and probably daydreaming about being the first twelve-year-old to win an Oscar for Best Actress.

It's safe to say that my two best friends are used to my not-so-friendly competition with Max. From the moment he first strolled into Clarktown Elementary two years ago with his designer jeans and a massive ego (and grades to rival mine), it's been insta-hate between us. But what my friends don't get is that this time it's different. Today, my hard work and sweat will pay off. It all comes down to this moment.

Mr. Orwell is about to hand back our reports on Greek mythology.

"Breathe, Lily," Lauren murmurs. "You look like you're going to pass out." I'm surprised she doesn't check my pulse. Lauren is the caretaker in our friend group. She's been bandaging up neighborhood kids and rescuing stray animals for as long as I've known her—fearless in the face of blood or tall trees with kittens trapped in them.

Kelli sighs. "You do this *every* time. I mean, it's just a report."

Yeah, right. Like she would ever say that the outfits she carefully plans every day were "just" clothes. But she's saved me from countless fashion disasters (like a purple polka-dotted sweater paired with a plaid skirt), so I keep my snarky thoughts to myself.

Without taking my eyes off Max, I say, "This report is our first big middle school assignment. *And* Mr. Orwell grades in percentages, not just letter grades." But I can't bring myself to tell them the real reason I'm sticky with nervous sweat about this assignment.

"Your point is . . . what exactly?" Kelli asks.

"Lily means that she's going to fight Max for a one-point difference in their grades," Lauren explains, "instead of pouting over another A-plus grade identical to Max's."

"See?" I spare a quick glance at my friends before resuming my staring contest with Max. "Lauren gets me."

Kelli looks like she wants to respond, but Mr. Orwell is coming down our row, so she just shakes her head at me.

Mr. Orwell puts my report facedown on my desk. Ten pages of typed, double-spaced paper, barely held together despite all my efforts with my mom's industrial-strength stapler.

"Excellent work, Lily!" he says. "I especially liked the extra touch of including a Greek pantheon family tree!"

Okay, maybe the family tree detailing every single messy relationship between the gods and goddesses, complete with full-color illustrations—was a *tiny* bit overkill. But better safe than sorry. With shaking hands, I flip over my paper.

A *100%* is in red ink at the top of the paper.

Yes! Take that, Max Zhang! All the hours I put into that report were *totally* worth it if it means beating Max. Mr. Orwell even wrote *I love this!!!* next to the family tree. I must have really knocked it out of the park if I got three exclamation points—and bonus that it's underlined!

But wait a minute . . . I flip through the pages to make sure I didn't miss Mr. Orwell's comments, but nothing's there. My hand shoots into the air even though he's still standing right next to me. "What about the extra credit?" I ask.

That's the real reason my stomach is all tied up in knots. The Film. I've never shared my films with anyone except Lauren and Kelli, and I'm desperate to know what Mr. Orwell thought of *The Tragic Romance of Medusa*— my twenty-minute original film. Maybe a retelling of the Medusa myth as an epic romance wasn't exactly what he had in mind when he said we could turn in a "brief supplementary video" for extra credit. What if it sucked? Doubt crawls along my skin. *My dream to be a filmmaker is going to die in seventh-grade Honors English class.*

"A hundred percent is the most you can get," Mr. Orwell says with a smile. "The extra credit was to boost your written report grade, which you didn't need. You would have gotten a hundred, with or without the video."

For once, I don't care about the points. I open my mouth to ask about my film, but I'm rudely interrupted.

"Nerd!" Max coughs into his elbow.

Mr. Orwell frowns. "No need for name-calling." With a name like Orwell and what must be a lifetime of *Animal Farm* and *1984* jokes, our teacher is, understandably, a little sensitive about name-calling.

"Sorry," Max says, looking all fake innocent. "I didn't mean that *Lily* was a nerd. Why would anyone think I meant her?"

"You should talk!" I glare at Max. "Didn't you make a mobile of all eight planets, plus Pluto, for the space unit project last year?"

"Lily," Mr. Orwell says warningly before moving down the aisle.

Kelli peers over my shoulder at my paper. "See? You were worrying over nothing."

But Lauren isn't looking at my paper. She's staring at me. "Did you turn in a film for the video extra credit?"

I flush. "Yes." I don't have to add anything more. We've all been friends since kindergarten and know everything there is to know about each other.

"Oh!" Kelli's eyes light up with understanding. "That's why you wanted to do that Medusa film!" Her hand goes to her scalp, and she winces. The plastic snakes we attached to her hair were a nightmare to get out. "I should have known."

"Me too." Lauren smiles at me. She played the part of Poseidon so she doesn't have painful memories of plastic snakes stubbornly stuck to her hair. "Lily, this is perfect! You're always making films about myths and fairy tales anyway, so of course you'd make a film for the mythology unit!" Then her face scrunches up. "But why didn't you tell us what you were planning?"

"I don't know." I'm not usually shy but turning in that film took every ounce of bravery I had. "Can we talk about this later?" I mutter. The last thing I need is for Max to know how much an extra-credit video means to me, and speaking of my pain-in-the-butt rival . . .

Max is just now getting his own paper from Mr. Orwell. *Please get a ninety-nine. Please get a ninety-nine,* I chant silently to myself.

My friends don't quite understand my feud with Max, but they've been on my side from the beginning. And when I say beginning, I mean when he moved to town two years ago.

My jaw tenses at the memory. There I was—totally focused on winning a pizza party for my fifth-grade class in the school's One Thousand Books Reading Challenge and blissfully unaware that everything was about to change. My friends tease me about tackling every academic competition like I'm going for the gold in the Olympics, but what can I say? My passion is real.

Then, one day into the challenge, Max strolled into class and handed in *four* summaries of Goosebumps books (good series but short books) before I had a chance to finish the eight hundred and forty pages of the last book in a young adult fantasy series (good series but *long* books). It was clear that I had underestimated Max, but to be fair, how was I supposed to know that the new kid, with his trendy clothes and too-cool attitude, was a serious contender?

It still makes me burn to think of the moment that Ms. Morrison put four yellow smiley-face stickers next to Max's name on the reading bulletin board and then turned to me, saying, "I thought you'd be the first one on the board, Lily, but it looks like you have competition." Her words were like a dagger to my heart.

On his way back to his seat, Max smirked at the thick, heavy tome on my desk (seriously, what was I thinking—there are encyclopedias shorter than this book) and said, "Huh. Interesting strategy. Good thing I showed up."

That's why Max Zhang and I are destined to be archenemies forever.

Max is finally turning over his paper, but it's with mind-numbing slowness. Of course, he knows I'm watching him, so he's going to draw out my torment by moving at the speed of an injured snail. He glances at the grade, and then meets my eyes. Smugly, he mouths, *One. Hundred. Percent.*

Noooooo! Hot anger rushes through me as I flash back to Max taking credit for winning us the fifth-grade pizza party even though I read *almost* as many books as he did, and (this is the important part) I did it without stooping to his arguably unethical strategy of reading only short books. "It's not fair! I worked hard on that report!" Oops. Did I say that out loud?

"You got a hundred too," Lauren reminds me.

I guess I did say it out loud. Still, Lauren has a point. I shouldn't get distracted by Max. I should be panicking over the fact that Mr. Orwell didn't say anything *at all* about my film.

Mr. Orwell finishes passing out the papers and returns to the front of the class. "Okay, everyone! I have a very special announcement!" He's full-on beaming. "As you know, I offered an extra-credit video option for this mythology report."

I sit up straighter, and my heart beats faster.

"One of you, in particular, did an amazing job and went above and beyond the requirements."

Is he talking about me? Then my gaze slides over to Max, and his smug smile stops my heart cold.

That mobile of the solar system he did last year was

mechanized—as in the planets were timed to revolve around the sun in a perfect elliptical and spin in place to mimic each planet's daily cycle. What if he did some kind of "how to build a robot Kraken" video for extra credit?

"A film!" Mr. Orwell says, and my heart soars. *It has to be me.* No way did Max make an actual film. He's not creative enough. "A film so powerful that I couldn't resist showing it to the principal. She agrees with me that the film needs to be shared with the Clarktown community. As a result, we're publishing it on the school website!"

Lauren and Kelli look at me excitedly, and I can hardly breathe at the thought of *my* film on the school website. This is almost as cool as winning the school district's annual Clarktown's Got Talent video competition, but let's face it—that would take a miracle.

Every year, the school district puts on a cutthroat contest between Clarktown's elementary school, middle school, and high school. We're talking Oscars-intense award ceremonies, but instead of gold statues and acceptance speeches, our school district competition has losing kids screaming and crying as they're carried away by adults. The high schoolers, of course, are too cool to cry and too big to be carried. Not that it matters because the high schoolers almost always win. The elementary school kids have to settle for the rare occasion when the overwhelming cuteness of their videos score them a win. Like that one year in first grade when a kindergarten teacher put her whole class in Pikachu hats and recorded them playing *Pokémon Go*. But the middle school videos never win.

"And now for a sneak preview," Mr. Orwell says, interrupting my thoughts. He laughs a little at his own joke before going to the computer and turning on the projector.

I'm shivering with anticipation. Not to brag, but the opening scene with Medusa drying her pre-snake hair in my bathroom while Poseidon rises out of the tub accompanied by strains of Lizzo's "Truth Hurts" is genius.

Then the video starts . . .

And it's not my film.

Instead, the screen is filled with jarring camerawork and fleeting images of dark, sharp corners. What the heck? The camera pans out to show a rat, equipped with a tiny camera on its back, racing through a maze. *This is a mistake.* Any minute now, Mr. Orwell is going to say, "Oops! Wrong video!"

But then a sound from my nightmares soars through the speakers—except this is more horrible than anything I could have imagined, so I can't actually be dreaming.

It's Max in voice-over, narrating *his film*. "Modern-day humans are not so different from the ancient Greek heroes trapped in the Minotaur's labyrinth."

My stomach turns sour. In fact, I may actually throw up.

There's a dramatic pause as the rat rounds a corner

and pounces on a hunk of cheese. "We are all rats in a maze," Max says, like he's revealing the secret of the universe.

You. Have. Got. To. Be. Kidding.

TWO

"'EDGY AND BRILLIANT!'" I WAIL. That's what Mr. Orwell called Max's stupid, pretentious film. "I can't believe *his* film is going on the school website!"

My friends have been listening to me rant all the way from sixth period art class to the school theater. Clarktown is a mostly white and middle-class town an hour outside liberal Seattle, and it's so small that there's just one elementary school, one middle school, and one high school—all in the same three-block radius and all sharing the same theater.

Kelli's face shines with outrage. "Our film was way better!" My leading actress is taking this personally. "There weren't even any actors in his film."

I kick the ground in disgust. "Not unless you count the rat in *Of Mice and Mazes.*" I'm not kidding—that's what Max actually called his film.

"Mr. Orwell just didn't get the feminist message in our film," Lauren says with a sigh. My activist-minded creative consultant is also taking this personally.

"He said our film was 'unrealistic'!" Maybe all my films *do* have supernatural or fantasy themes, but I'd rather make a feminist mythical romance than some broody twelve-year-old take on the meaning of life.

"That's ridiculous!" says Kelli loyally. "I mean, Max's robot Minotaur at the end was kind of cool, but it definitely wasn't realistic."

"Mr. Orwell didn't actually say our film was unrealistic," Lauren says.

True. But what he *had* said, when I stayed after class to ask for feedback, was actually kind of worse.

"Your film was . . . uh . . . very creative," he said, fiddling with a pen, "and if you're wondering why I chose Max's film, it's just that his film was such a powerful mirror of real life."

Right. "Because Max's film about a rat in a maze from the *rat's point of view* totally came from his real-life experience," I blurted out.

Mr. Orwell got a pained look on his face and said, "The rat was a metaphor, Lily."

Like I didn't know that. But Mr. Orwell was one hundred percent wrong.

Max is a literal rat.

Lauren waves a hand in front of my eyes. "Hello? Lily,

are you okay? You're muttering about rats."

I blink and come back to the present. "Let's face it," I say bitterly. "We can't afford rich-kid tricks like a rodent-sized camera or a robot Minotaur." *The Tragic Romance of Medusa*, like all my films, was shot and edited on the tablet I got from my parents in exchange for a promise of unlimited little brother babysitting. Our budget for the film basically covered a bag of plastic snakes from the dollar store, a can of fake-stone spray paint, and a costume pitchfork repurposed as a trident.

My steps slow as we approach the theater. "Maybe this isn't such a good idea."

Lauren and Kelli take my arms and steer me toward the main doors.

"It's *your* idea, and it's brilliant," Lauren says firmly.

"You can't back out now," Kelli says. "I already quit drama club!"

I don't point out that she was going to quit anyway. The drama club is supposed to be open to every student, but the high school kids are the ones who run it, and they always refuse to cast Kelli, the only middle schooler in the club, as anything but an extra. The last straw was last week's drama club audition for the Clarktown's Got Talent video competition.

Normally, Kelli wouldn't have expected to be cast as anything but an extra, but this year's entry was going to be a video of the drama club's *The Sound of Music* production. Kelli really thought she had a shot at the part of one of the von Trapp children. After all, she can act *and* sing better than most of the high schoolers. Unfortunately, they cast her as a goat instead.

That's when I got the idea to enter a film into the competition. Every year, the middle school kids put together a few half-hearted videos to battle it through the competition, but this year was going to be different. I was determined to score a historically epic win for Clarktown Middle School and highlight our under-appreciated talents while we were at it. I'd get to make films, Kelli would get a lead role, and Lauren would get to deliver progressive political messages. So what if the high school's sophisticated productions or the adorable elementary school kids always scoop up the prize? I wasn't about to let a little thing like "It's never been done before" scare me off. Or that's what I thought then.

"I don't know what I was thinking!" I dig my heels into the ground, but my friends just pull harder. "No middle school entry has even come close to winning. Remember that seventh grader who did the hot dog–eating video last year? Losing the competition was so traumatic that he won't even talk about it!"

And I should know because I interviewed past middle school contenders to prepare for the competition. Their interviews flash before my eyes now. The skateboard video kid. The kid who did an interpretive dance of the "circle of life." The stand-up comedy kid. None of them have won, but I was going to change that by making a film so awesome that they'd *have* to give our middle school entry the prize.

But that was before my spirit was crushed by Mr. Orwell, Max, and *Of Mice and Mazes*.

"That kid wasn't traumatized because he lost the competition." Lauren grimaces. "It had more to do with the two dozen hot dogs he threw up."

"On camera," Kelli adds with a shudder. The entire school auditorium erupted into shrieks and a unified "Gross!" when *that* video was shown in the first round of the competition. Obviously, it was immediately eliminated.

It was undoubtedly disgusting, but that's not the part that I get hung up on. "I don't get why he couldn't take two minutes to edit out the throwing up part. I mean, it's not like he was eating the hot dogs live." Mom told me that the Clarktown's Got Talent competition started out as an actual talent show, but then a routine went sideways (involving an overeager dog with an overactive bladder), so the school district made it a video competition instead, and it's been that way ever since.

"That's what I'm trying to tell you." Lauren's grip tightens on my shoulder. "You're not just some kid who filmed himself inhaling a bunch of hot dogs. You are an *actual* filmmaker, and if you can't win this contest for our school, then no one can."

The faith in her eyes makes my throat go dry, and if it weren't for my friends dragging me forward, I'd be tempted to turn and run.

"You finished the script for the new film, right?" Lauren asks, eyeing my backpack as she drops my arm to open the door.

"Yeah." My stomach flutters with nerves. We put up an audition call flyer at our middle school last week, and today is when we're holding auditions. "Did I mention that it's a really rough draft?"

Kelli tugs on my arm. "I'm sure it's great! My character is still a vampire slayer, right?"

"*Activist* vampire slayer," Lauren says. "And I'm still the slayer's mentor, right?"

The truth is—I *am* proud of the way I wrote these roles. It's not as easy as it might seem to write a screenplay for a political satire meets *Buffy the Vampire Slayer* retelling. . . .

"Yes," I say, my spirits starting to lift. "Kelli, you're Summer Bouffant, high school student by day and slayer by night. And Lauren, you're Jillian Rupert, community organizer by day and the slayer's mentor by night."

"Excellent!" Kelli's eyes glow with excitement, and she tightens her hold.

I pull my arm from Kelli's grip. "Do you think anyone will show up to our audition?" Sharing the screenplay with my friends is one thing, but sharing it with other kids, who might hate it, is completely different.

Lauren gestures at the bulletin board next to the entrance. "It's not like there are many options." She's right. The only thing on the board, other than our own audition call, is a shiny black-and-red artsy flyer for dance auditions being held in the prop room.

"That's new," I say, pointing at the flyer. "Someone should remind them that the interpretive dance video was eliminated in the first round last year." The video was done by a middle schooler, of course.

Kelli barely glances at the flyer. Dance is kind of a sore spot with her. She's an amazing actor and singer, but her lack of dance skills keeps her from being a triple threat onstage. "Stop stalling, Lily!"

"We want everyone to know how talented you are." Lauren has a determined expression on her face that I know all too well. She's normally easygoing, but there's no stopping her when she has an idea in her head. "Am I going to have to make you go in?"

She would too. Last year, Lauren talked me into joining her quest to get more diverse books into the Clarktown library. It took four emails, a total of three meetings with two different librarians, and a forty-five-minute Power-Point presentation, but in the end, the library bought all the books we recommended *and* put Lauren in charge of the children's book display for Black History Month and me for Asian American and Pacific Islander Heritage Month. In other words, there's no giving up as far as Lauren is concerned.

"I'm never going to get a starring role if you don't direct this film," Kelli says, blinking her big green eyes at me. She won't let me back out either.

The palms of my hands grow damp. If my film sucks, Max will mock me mercilessly. On the other hand, he'll mock me no matter what I do. Plus, I'll never forgive myself if I let Max, of all people, ruin this for me.

"Okay, let's do this." I throw back my shoulders and push open the main doors.

Then my mouth falls open . . . because the lobby is crowded with kids.

Twenty kids for five parts—three supporting roles and two extras.

I should be freaking out, but an eerie calm falls over me as I step onstage with copies of the audition scenes in one hand and a mic in the other. Who cares if they don't like the film? That's their problem because *The Chosen One Slays Big Business on the Hellmouth* is awesome.

"Attention, everyone!" I call out. Kelli and Lauren are standing on either side of me, and my confidence rises. "As the casting call said, we're looking for three people to play supporting roles of the main villain and the two best friends of the slayer. We also need extras to play vampires, cheerleaders—"

I break off abruptly as I spot a familiar figure walking by the open doors of the theater.

No way! He'll ruin *everything*.

I shove the audition scenes into Kelli's startled hands and pass Lauren the mic, then call out over my shoulder, "I'll be right back! Take over for a minute, okay?"

"Where are you going?" Lauren must have forgotten she was holding the mic because she says it so loudly that she gets a burst of static feedback.

I'm already hurtling down the steps from the stage and running up the aisle.

I catch him just outside the doors. "Max Zhang!" I pant, slightly out of breath from my mad dash. "Don't you dare even think about auditioning for my film!"

He turns around, eyes widening. "What film?"

"Don't pretend you don't know!" I jab a finger at his chest. "You're trying to get a part in my film so you can say awful things like, 'Oh, isn't the slayer *adorable*.'"

He shakes his head. "Trust me when I say that I have *no* idea what you're talking about."

"Oh, yeah? Then what are you doing here?"

The Zhangs are rich developers responsible for building the new gated community where Max now lives, and the gossip is that the Royal Palisades has its own private clubhouse, tennis court, and swimming pool. So why would Max be slumming it at our little school theater?

To sabotage my film—that's why.

Max's eyes shift away from mine. "I just happened to be here. That's all."

"Right. At the *exact* same time we're holding auditions for our film." My voice drips sarcasm. "What a coincidence."

"I don't care about your stupid film!" His hands ball into fists.

Whoa. Where did *that* come from? Sneering put-downs are more Max's style. Rage yelling is my thing.

We stare at each other for a silent beat, and then Max uncurls his fingers. His mouth curves into his signature smirk, but it seems half-hearted. "Why would I want to audition for your film? Mr. Orwell chose *my* film to put on the school website, remember?"

It's not like I could forget. Scalding heat rushes into my face. "Your film sucks." Not my best comeback, I admit. I fully expect Max to mock my subpar insult, but he just shrugs.

Um, what's happening? It's not like him to leave me hanging like this. This weirdly passive Max is freaking me out. Determined to get a rise from him, I say, "It's pretentious and . . . derivative."

"Pretentious?" A small fire sparks in his eyes. "Says the girl who just used the word *derivative* to describe my film. Do you even know what that means, or did you just pick that from your 'word of the week' calendar?"

That's more like it—this is the Max I know. "Derivative," I say firmly. "It means copying other things and being unable to have an original thought if your life depended on it. It means stealing from every Discovery Channel documentary you've ever watched. It means being a sheep—you know, like the ones you were drawing in art class."

"Those were horses!"

"Not according to Ms. Chase." My art teacher has my undying adoration for mistaking Max's unnecessarily fluffy horses for sheep. Anticipation fills me as I rise on my toes, ready to counter his next insult, but it doesn't come.

"Goodbye." He turns and starts to walk away.

That's it? I can't believe he's going to leave without trying to get the last word in. Something is off about Max, and come to think of it, isn't he supposed to be on his way to that snooty Chinese school in the city right now? Yeah, that's suspicious, all right. "Why are you here?" I shout after him.

He doesn't pause or turn around. "You're so weird, Lily."

"That's still not an answer!"

But he rounds the corner and is already out of sight.

THREE

THE AUDITIONS HAVE WRAPPED UP, and Kelli, Lauren, and I are just starting to sit down on the stage to decide our cast when the high schoolers (dressed in nun habits, flowery dresses with aprons, and lederhosen) burst into the theater.

Kelli jumps to her feet. "Hey! We booked the theater already."

"Nope." A tall teenage boy in lederhosen strides up to the stage. "We have the theater for *Sound of Music* rehearsal right now."

On cue, a girl in an apron starts yodeling. *Ugh.* High school method acting is the worst. They must have worn those costumes all day during their classes. Unfortunately, as annoying as the high schoolers are, they're also right.

Lauren and I lock eyes in a silent exchange.

You tell her.

No, you tell her.

You do it.

I break eye contact first, which means I'm on the hook for breaking the bad news. Darn Lauren and her uncanny ability to not blink.

"Kelli?" I clear my throat. "I was only able to book the theater until four." Honestly, we were lucky that the high school gets out an hour later than our middle school. Otherwise, they would have snatched up the three to four time slot too.

"What?" Kelli shrieks. "An hour isn't enough time!" And this is why we didn't want to tell her.

"Calm down," Lauren says. "It's better than nothing."

"And we're not filming here anyway," I remind her. "We just need the theater for auditions and rehearsals."

"Hey," the tall teen says to Kelli, "aren't you supposed to play our goat?"

Lauren and I grab Kelli's arms before she can leap off the stage and attack him.

"Sorry," I pant, pinning her arm behind her back. "She's just, uh, method acting for her role as the slayer."

"Activist slayer," Lauren corrects me.

"Whatever," the teen says. "Look, can you hurry up and clear out? We don't have much time to rehearse for the competition."

Kelli almost wrenches my arm out of its socket, lurching forward.

The yodeling girl stops singing just then; as a result, Kelli's voice soars through the theater, loud and clear. "We're entering the video competition too, and we're going to win!" She really does have a voice for the stage.

There's a split second of silence, and then all the high schoolers burst into laughter. The tall guy is laughing so hard that he's bent over. "You actually think you can win?"

"Aw, let them try," the yodeling girl says. "It's cute." She turns to Kelli. "You can still be our goat if you want to be a part of a *real* act."

I can feel Kelli's arm shake, and it's like there's a conduit from her body to mine, filling me with anger too. How dare they cast her as a goat and then *laugh* at her? "My friend is way more talented than all of you, and she's right. We *are* going to win."

"Yeah, we are," Lauren says staunchly.

Our heads held high, we scoop up our backpacks and bags of plastic stakes and vampire fangs, and stalk out of the theater with the laughter still following us out.

"Can you believe they cast that teenager as Kurt?" Kelli fumes, pushing open the exit doors of the theater building. "He must be seven feet tall, his voice is deeper than my dad's, and he can't carry a tune or act to save his life!"

She tried out for all the von Trapp children roles, including Kurt.

"I know," Lauren says, "but we should focus on our film. We still need to decide on the roles."

"Let's go to the community center," I say. "We can use one of the Chinese school classrooms." My family runs Hong Chinese Academy out of the basement of the Clarktown Community Center. It's kind of my second home.

Lauren nods. "That's a good idea. You're supposed to pick up your little brother from Minecraft Club at the center anyway, right?"

"Yeah." My feet are already turning in the direction of the center. "I always have to drag Daniel away from his gaming buddies, so he won't mind staying a little longer while we talk about casting."

Kelli sighs. "It's not the theater, but I guess the community center is fine."

It's only five blocks away from our school, so less than ten minutes later, we're approaching the dingy white-and-blue building with its weedy parking lot.

"Is it my imagination, or has it gotten even more run-down since I was last here?" Kelli asks.

Lauren looks around. "I think you're right."

"It just needs a little new paint and some weeding," I say defensively. Kelli took kid drama classes here, and Lauren's activist parents hold community meetings

26

here sometimes, but the center doesn't mean as much to them. As for me, I've taken a lot of classes and joined just about every club at the center (but not Minecraft Club—Daniel can have that, thank you very much), and that doesn't even count the summers and Saturdays for Chinese school. Plus, there's all the family time spent cleaning classrooms, organizing folders, and labeling bins for the Chinese school. Now that I think about it, I've probably spent more time at the Clarktown Community Center than my own house.

"I don't think I've been here since the storm last winter," Kelli says. That's when most of Clarktown lost electricity, and half the town ended up at the community center, which had backup generators. "Mayor Richman got so mad when Lily organized that scavenger hunt to entertain the little kids and put 'something from the mayor' on the list."

"I didn't tell them to take his toupee!" I say.

Lauren raises an eyebrow. "No, but I distinctly remember you telling them to 'be creative.' I mean, these were preschoolers. What did you think was going to happen?"

"Ooh, I remember that," Kelli says. "Clarktown hasn't had so much excitement since the center got flooded a few years back."

My heart wrenches when I remember my family standing in the community center basement, staring at the wreck that was our Chinese school. Even now, I can still smell the stink of mildew and feel my feet sinking into the soggy carpets.

"It was cool how everyone turned up to help clean up afterward," Lauren says with a glance at me.

It's true. Even now, I get a warm glow at the thought of all those people showing up with trash bags and mops. Even Mayor Richman came right away and waded into the muck to help, not even stopping to put on his toupee. I smile at the memory. "Yeah, the center has been through a lot."

As we walk down the hallway, I automatically check the bulletin board. There's a flyer advertising piano lessons, a wanted ad for a nanny, and a flyer for a dance club in the same artsy style as the one at the theater. In other words, there's nothing much going on in Clarktown except that someone is trying to start a dance club.

At the main desk, Ms. Moreno is frowning at a sheet of paper, and there are deep lines on her forehead. When she spots us, she quickly shoves the paper into a drawer. "Hello, girls!" Her family owns the community center, and she used to be the center's director until her kids insisted that she finally retire last year at the age of seventy-three or, as she calls it, "seventy-three years young." So now Ms. Moreno volunteers at the reception desk. "Are you here to pick up Daniel, Lily?"

"Not yet. Can I have the key to the school? We need to use—"

"Hey!" Kelli breaks in excitedly. "I just remembered that the center has an auditorium. Remember, Lily? Our summer drama camp performance was there."

"Oh, that's right," I say. "I almost forgot about *The Wizard of Clarktown*." I was the Tin Girl, and my wooden performance (or maybe metallic is the more appropriate description) at age seven was my last attempt at acting, but that was also when Kelli, in the role of Dorothy, got bitten by the acting bug.

"Maybe we can have rehearsals in the auditorium," Kelli says.

"Rehearsals?" Ms. Moreno asks with a puzzled wrinkle in her forehead.

"We're entering a film for Clarktown's Got Talent," Lauren tells her. "*The Chosen One Slays Big Business on the Hellmouth*. Lily is the writer and director, Kelli is the star, and I'm the creative consultant."

"Isn't that nice." Ms. Moreno's smile doesn't seem as bright as usual. "But I'm sorry that I can't let you use the auditorium. It's booked every day in the afternoons."

"Really?" That's weird. The only things that happen in the auditorium are the drama camp performances and preschool singalongs.

"I'm surprised you haven't heard about it, Lily." Ms. Moreno sounds like her cheerful self, so maybe I was imagining things earlier.

Before I can ask her what she means, the door behind

her opens, and three women come out of the back office. Ms. Leticia (who's Ms. Moreno's daughter), Lauren's mother, and my mom.

Normally, I wouldn't have given it a second thought, but the three of them don't usually hang out together, and then there was Ms. Moreno's odd behavior. . . . Well, let's just say it's enough to make me pay attention.

Ms. Moreno turns around. "All done?"

"You could have joined us, Mom." Ms. Leticia sounds tired. She's the interim director even though she already has the job of running the center's dual-language Spanish and English preschool. According to my parents, the Moreno family can't afford to hire a full-time director, so Ms. Leticia has to do it.

"Someone needs to be at the reception desk." Ms. Moreno smiles at us. "After all, if kids come in, needing a place to rehearse—"

"Mom, what are you doing here?" I ask in a rush, my tongue tripping over the words. I'm not sure why I don't want to tell Mom about the film yet. It's not like she would stop me from entering the video competition, but my parents don't get why film is so important to me.

Mom looks at me strangely. "Where else would I be?"

Good question. Mom's always here. As principal of our Chinese school, she does all the communication, accounting, publicity, and clerical stuff, and even though our school is only on Saturdays, she uses her amazing principal skills to help out at the center the rest of the week too.

Then Mom's gaze shifts to Ms. Leticia and Lauren's mom, and I could *swear* she looks guilty. My skin prickles with suspicion.

"Mom, are you and Dad holding a meeting?" Lauren asks excitedly. "Why didn't you tell me?" Ms. Carter is a civil rights lawyer, and Mr. Carter is the director of the Clarktown food bank. They're both community organizers and sometimes hold meetings at the center.

"No meeting today," her mother replies.

Lauren visibly deflates. She's the only person I know who would be upset about missing a planning meeting to picket a detention center or sue a slumlord, but this is the girl who has a picture of her first parent-daughter protest march hanging in her locker. She was six months old and strapped to her mom in an Ergo decorated with a sign that said, "Baby Feminist."

A puzzled frown creases Lauren's forehead. "Then why are you here?"

"I just stopped by . . . to visit Sara."

Huh. I've known Lauren and her family all my life because our dads have been best friends since college, but my mom and Ms. Carter don't usually hang out unless it's part of a family thing.

"Thanks for coming, Janet," Mom says to Ms. Carter.

"Yes, thank you both," Ms. Leticia adds. "It was good to talk."

Okay, what's going on here? My mom and Ms. Leticia always seemed to be more work friends than anything else. Why are they all hanging out suddenly for no reason? Come to think of it—Mom has been all weird and tense lately. Not that she would ever say anything to me about it.

Worry creeps up my spine as Mom exchanges secretive looks with Ms. Carter, Ms. Leticia, and Ms. Moreno. *Something is wrong.*

And the adults aren't telling us what it is.

FOUR

KELLI, LAUREN, AND I PULL together three small desks in the Chinese school classroom, and Lauren starts us off. "Should we cast Suzie as a vampire or a cheerleader? I'm thinking vampire."

"I see her as a cheerleader, actually. She's got that vibe," Kelli says.

"Then we should cast against type." Lauren turns to me. "What do you think, Lily?"

That's an easy one. "Vampire Cheerleader. Obviously."

Kelli's mouth falls open. "Why didn't I think of that? I have a great idea for a vampire cheerleader costume!"

"I love it!" Lauren agrees. "It's so subversive!"

Even though the three of us have been friends forever, we haven't always had a lot in common. That all changed last year when we discovered *Buffy the Vampire Slayer*. Now we are a sisterhood of diehard slayerettes. We even saved up our allowance money to buy *Buffy* fan jewelry. Lauren has silver earrings of the scythe Buffy used on the show, Kelli has a Sunnydale High School class ring, and I have the Symbol of Anyanka—the green gem amulet that gives the vengeance demon her powers.

Kelli is making us all cosplay outfits for Comic Con next month—which is another thing I haven't gotten around to telling my parents. They'll end up letting me go, but they'll probably be all judgy about it. Dad will say it sounds like a waiguoren thing. A *foreigner* thing. That's what he calls everything he thinks is strange and American. Mom, on the other hand, has lived in the United States since she was around my age. So she won't call Comic Con a waiguoren thing. She'll call it a "white people" thing.

And if I point out that both Lauren and I are into Comic Con, and *we're* not white, she'll just say, "You two are the exception that proves the rule." Whatever that means.

Kelli walks over to the whiteboard and starts putting up what we've decided so far. We all agreed on Marissa as the teenage witch best friend of the slayer, and we've also decided on Suzie and Chelsea as the two extras, but we're stuck on the other two roles. The villain and the ordinary best friend.

As Kelli scribbles on the board, I pick absently at a random piece of tape stuck to my desk. The tape finally comes loose, but a piece of the desk (which was apparently held in place by the tape) springs free and smacks my hand. "Ow!" I yell. Our school could really use a furniture upgrade, and new paint wouldn't hurt either.

Without missing a beat, Lauren opens her backpack, takes out a roll of tape, and tapes the flapping plastic back to the rest of the desk.

I glare at the desk. "The furniture has never been the same since we used it to barricade the door against the Knitting League ghost."

Kelli pauses in her work at the whiteboard. "I'm sorry. What?"

Even Lauren, who's never fazed, looks puzzled.

"It was during an overnight Chinese school camp," I say with a shrug. "I think I was eight."

"I keep telling you that it doesn't count as camping when you pitch tents *inside* the community center," Kelli says.

"We roasted the marshmallows *outside*."

"Where outside? In the forest? By a babbling brook?"

"In the parking lot," I mumble.

Lauren shakes her head. "Lily mentions a Knitting League ghost, and you're fixated on where she roasted marshmallows?" She gestures to me. "Continue, please."

"There's not much to tell. Someone was telling scary stories about the Knitting League ghost—"

Kelli interrupts me. "And that someone was . . . ?"

"Fine. It was me." I mean, what's a campout (even an indoor one) if it doesn't have ghost stories?

"There we go." Kelli gives a satisfied nod.

"*Anyway*, we heard a noise, so we panicked and barricaded the door with the furniture. It turns out it wasn't a ghost—it was my parents, and they weren't thrilled to find themselves on the other side of the barricade."

"I see." Lauren calmly goes back to editing my script. Kelli rolls her eyes and puts a smiley face next to a name on the whiteboard.

I take a peek at Lauren's edits. So far, she's written, *Summer needs more agency here* and *Demon businessman explaining master plan to Summer before unleashing demons from the Hellmouth is too much. Delete scene?* She's right about the first edit, but dead wrong about the second one.

"He has to give at least one evil exposition speech," I protest.

"But does he have to do it while Summer's friends are escaping behind his back? He's supposed to be an evil genius. You'd think he'd just level the town instead of getting distracted by bantering with the slayer."

She might be right. "Okay, I won't have her friends escape behind the smart demon's back." I make a note on the script. "But villains are *always* willing to trade insults with the hero while describing their plan for world domination in great detail, so the rest of the scene stays."

"Sure," Lauren says easily. "You're the director." That's why she's the only one who is allowed to edit my script. Kelli has a good eye, but she gets . . . passionate about arguing her opinions when it comes to theater.

Kelli is now putting smiley faces, frowning faces, and the occasional heart next to the kids' names and the parts they auditioned for. She steps back to look at her handiwork, almost tripping over my backpack. "We'd have more room if we were in the theater," she grumbles. She's clearly still mad about the high schoolers kicking us out.

"There are bigger rooms upstairs," I say. "In fact, I was thinking we should do our filming in the community center."

Kelli frowns. "I thought you were going to talk to Principal Watson about filming at our school."

"Yeah, about that . . ." I start fiddling with the tape again. "She said it didn't sound 'school appropriate.'"

Lauren looks up from her notebook. She knows what I'm like when I get carried away. "You went into too much detail, didn't you?"

Fine. Maybe it wasn't totally necessary to mention the plastic axe and fake blood.

"Lily!" Kelli glares at me. "Our film is supposed to be at a school." She looks around at the brightly colored "Year of the Tiger" banners and stroke order charts.

My chest grows tight. It feels weird to have my friends in my Chinese school, and suddenly, I see it through their eyes. The run-down furniture and Chinese characters everywhere.

"This *is* a school," I say defensively.

"But we need a *high school* set," Kelli clarifies.

Ah. I squirm in my kid-sized desk, and my gaze goes to the crayon drawings on the walls. The one I did of my house with all the rooms labeled in Chinese has a crooked purple roof, and my bedroom is definitely too big to be in proportion to the rest of the house. I'm glad my name is in Chinese so my friends can't identify that drawing as mine. "Okay, point taken."

"What about filming at the actual high school?" Kelli must really not want to film at the center to bring up this suggestion again.

"We've been through this already," Lauren says. "They won't let their competitors in the video competition use their school as a set."

"The center actually would be perfect." My eyes narrow in thought. "There's a long hallway outside the Fencing Team practice room that would work for our battles and chase scenes. I'm sure Ms. Moreno will let us film there." Note to self—don't mention slayer props and blood in my pitch to Ms. Moreno.

Lauren's pencil falls from her fingers. "Uh, that sounds good." *Is she blushing?* "Yeah, let's film there . . . outside the Fencing Team practice room."

Kelli and I both stare at her. What's going on?

Lauren avoids our eyes. "We can't cast Lincoln for the demon businessman," she says, pointing at the whiteboard, where Kelli has put a heart next to his name.

"Ha!" I pin her with a sharp gaze. "Do you think you can distract us that easily with such an obvious—"

"Why can't we cast Lincoln?" Kelli demands, capping her marker. "He totally looks the part!"

Okay, maybe Lauren *can* distract us that easily.

I don't admit it out loud, but I was picturing *Max* when I wrote the demon part. No one else looks quite as villainous. However, I did name our villain Maxistopheles Maxiavelli, so my friends have probably figured out that he's *loosely* based on Max.

"What do you not understand about Maxistopheles Maxiavelli being an evil genius!" Lauren throws up her hands in frustration. It was her idea to make our businessman villain a *literal* demon from the underworld. She's the creative consultant for a reason. "Lincoln just isn't believable as a scheming demon. Remember when he actually thought the rumor about my father being Anthony Mackie was true? I mean, have you met my dad?"

Lauren has a point. Mr. Carter is a great dad, but he's definitely not a cool action-hero movie star. The only person I know who tells cornier jokes is *my* dad.

Actually . . . Dad hasn't been making many jokes lately. The other day, I was passing a tub of margarine to

Mom, and I accidentally dropped it. I waited for Dad to say something, and when he didn't, *I* actually made the joke about having butterfingers. And he didn't even crack a smile. It's just not natural.

Suddenly, I'm thinking about Mom acting all cagey and weird earlier and having a secretive meeting with Ms. Carter and Ms. Leticia.

"Fine," Kelli is saying. "Maybe Lincoln isn't our demon, but he's not a bad actor." She taps the marker against her thigh as she studies the whiteboard. "How about this? Let's give Tim the Maxistopheles Maxiavelli part, and then we can cast Lincoln as Summer's clueless best friend."

"That could work," Lauren agrees. "Lily, what do you think?"

"Hmm?" I'm barely listening. "Oh, right. Yeah, sure."

Kelli frowns. "If you don't like Tim for the demon or Lincoln for the friend, just say so."

"The casting is fine." I set my tablet down. "Sorry. I was just thinking about seeing my mom earlier. I get the feeling she's hiding something from me."

"Really?" Lauren probably can't wrap her mind around the idea of parents keeping secrets from their kids. Her mom and dad are always telling her stuff like "Knowledge is power!"

"Why would she be hiding something from you?" Kelli asks. Her parents are like Lauren's—except for the whole "Knowledge is power" part, but they tell her *everything*. Her dad runs the town's ice cream parlor, and it's honestly shocking how much he overhears and repeats. Kelli is just like him. Her mom, the owner of a hair salon, likes to gossip too, but she's small-time compared to Kelli and her dad.

But my mom—her secrets don't even make sense.

Every year, someone sends us Lunar New Year presents. Dolls with silky black hair, a delicate tea set, velvet gloves, a red knit hat with bright pink roses, and—my favorite one—a beautifully illustrated book of Chinese myths. Mom just changes the subject whenever I ask where these gorgeous, perfect gifts come from. No, my friends won't understand. Why would they? *I* don't even understand.

Out loud, I say, "I guess I'm just being paranoid. I mean, this is Clarktown. What could happen here?"

I bet the residents of Sunnydale thought the same thing. Right before the Hellmouth opened up beneath their perfect little town.

FIVE

MOM TAKES THE GLASS JAR of pennies down from the top shelf of the pantry, and my stomach does a slow dive. It's weird that the sight of a repurposed mayonnaise jar filled with shiny copper coins makes me feel so queasy, but I know what those pennies mean. *Chinese school.*

"Can we talk about this penny punishment thing?" I ask as I put my empty cereal bowl in the sink. "I mean, if we want more kids to come to our school, making them literally pay for their mistakes might not be the way to go." What I *want* to say is that the other kids are ready to revolt over this new "owe a teacher a penny for every mistake you make on your homework" policy.

My parents came up with the idea a few weeks ago . . . and ever since then, I've been trying to explain why it's *not* a good idea. Hong Chinese Academy is our family business, and I don't want to see students fleeing for the exit over literal *pennies*.

Dad looks up from organizing colorful markers in his book bag. "It's not punishment." He zips up his bag. "It's encouragement." *Easy for him to say.* He teaches the five-to seven-year-olds, who are too young to be subjected to the public shaming that we older kids must endure. That's not quite how my parents put it, but that's what it boils down to.

"I get it," I say in my best imitation of the ultra-reasonable voice adults use when they're telling us kids something we don't want to hear. "But the other students are *already* less than thrilled about giving up four hours every Saturday and all summer for Chinese school."

"We want to show the parents that we take their kids' education seriously," Mom says, a line of tension creasing her forehead. "It's not the students who decide to come to our school. It's the parents. They're the ones we need to convince." Mom never used to worry about proving our school's value to the parents. But that was before the Zhangs showed up.

The first meeting between our mothers was almost as bad as my first meeting with Max. A little shiver crawls up my spine just thinking about it.

Basically, Mom had overheard Max speaking Mandarin to his mom in a grocery store. Sensing fresh blood, Mom went in for the kill—only to be told that Max already goes to a Chinese school with a more "academic focus." Apparently, his school does test prep and other rich-kid stuff.

I eye my mother sharply as a new thought enters my brain. Is that why Mom and Dad seem so stressed lately? Is our school losing students to some *Crazy Rich Asians* school in the city? I wouldn't be surprised. Max's parents are always bragging about his perfect Chinese. Anger makes my stomach clench because the run-down basement of the Clarktown Community Center can't possibly compete with a fancy big-city school.

Mom holds the mayonnaise-jar piggy bank out to my ten-year-old brother. "How many, Daniel?" A new homework policy isn't going to make our lights work or update the rickety classroom furniture or get rid of the smell of old carpet. But try telling my mother that.

With an evil grin directed at me, Daniel takes two measly pennies and puts them in his pocket—where they'll stay until laundry day. My irritating little brother doesn't make mistakes in copying his Chinese characters. He never leaves out a line or a dash, but Mom makes him take a few anyway. Just in case the unthinkable happens.

My pennies are definitely not just-in-case ones. Mom doesn't bother asking me how many I'll need. She just scoops out a generous handful, plunks them in a ziplock bag, and hands me about a dollar's worth of pennies.

"I'd have to get all the characters wrong to need that many!" I protest, but I take the bag because—let's face it—it could happen.

"Do you want Auntie Li asking me why you didn't bring enough pennies?" my mother asks calmly.

"No," I mutter. I can't imagine a worse fate than my teacher giving me what I call the Chinese stink eye of disappointment. Outside of school, my teacher is Auntie Li, Mom's BFF who bakes me cookies and listens to all my problems. But she turns into a whole different (and scary) person in the classroom. There, she's Laoshi. *Teacher.*

"Don't worry, Lily," Daniel chirps in a false-helpful voice. "I could spot you two more pennies if you need them." He dashes out of the kitchen before I can smack his arm.

Jerk. No one pushes my buttons like my little brother. Wait—that's not true. There *is* someone who's even more annoying than Daniel. Like teeth-gritting, fingernails-on-chalkboard annoying.

Obviously, I'm talking about Max Zhang.

With more force than necessary, I shove the heavy ziplock bag of pennies into the pocket of my jacket, feeling all lopsided from the weight. It will be much lighter after I turn in the homework, but this time, I won't forget to take the mostly empty bag out of my pocket. No way am I going to have a repeat of last week.

My face heats at the memory of racing down the halls to get to class on time and running smack into Max.

The impact knocked my breath out of my chest, sending books and folders flying everywhere. But that wasn't the worst part. *That* would be when a ziplock bag of pennies fell out of my jacket in one of those nightmarish slow-motion sequences . . . and crashed onto the floor with a jangly thud.

The sound seemed to echo down the hall forever, making my heart pound furiously. How was it possible that a few pennies could be so loud?

Max didn't even ask me if I was okay or help me pick up my stuff. He just pointed to my pennies and asked, "What's that? Lunch money?"

Everyone standing around thought his comment was hilarious. They all started laughing, and I thought I was going to die of embarrassment.

Then some random kid from school told Max all about the pennies and the new Chinese school rule. I just stood there, mouth hanging open and cheeks burning, realizing what must have happened. *Kelli.* Gossip is like air to that girl. I couldn't even blame her for blabbing about the pennies since I had never told her that it was supposed to be a secret, but you'd think she'd figure it out.

After Max heard about the pennies, he smirked and said, "Let me know if you need more pennies."

I'm not a violent person, but I wanted to punch that smug expression right off his face. Except I've never even remotely gotten in trouble before, so the chances that I was going to risk getting sent to the principal's office for fighting were exactly zero.

It was almost as bad when he called me "Lily Ping, Listen, Listen While I Sing" after the girl in the kindergarten Superkids reading program. To be fair, Max didn't join in when some other kids started yelling "Chong!" at me—to mimic the gong sound that ends Lily Ping's song about *L* sounds. In fact, he grew red in the face and looked like he regretted the whole thing, but it was still his fault in the first place. I've finally forgiven my parents for giving me the same name as *every single* fictional Chinese American girl, but I'll never forgive him.

Daniel comes back into the kitchen with his backpack bouncing on his skinny body and his thick glasses all crooked. "I need a snack for the car ride. Do we have any of those oatmeal chocolate granola bars left?" *Rookie mistake, little brother.* His eyes meet mine and widen in horror.

But I'm already in motion—and suddenly, we're dashing for the pantry. Normally, I'd let Daniel have the last granola bar since it's his favorite. Except there's the little matter of paying him back for his snarky comment about the pennies.

"No running in the house!" Dad looks up from the Chinese workbook he was reading at the kitchen table.

Mom just shakes her head.

My fingers close over the shiny foil of the bar a second before Daniel can get his hot, little hands on my prize. "Ha!" I yell triumphantly.

"It's not fair!" Daniel whines. "You didn't even want it."

I dangle the bar over his head as he tries to grab it. "What will you give me for it?"

"Lily, stop teasing your didi." Dad stands up, a warning look in his eyes.

Even more worrisome is that Mom is heading to the garage—where she keeps extra supplies of everything from toilet paper to cereal. Weren't those granola bars on sale last week? That would mean she bought extra boxes for sure.

Better wrap this up before I lose my bargaining chip. "Take my dishwashing shift tonight and the granola bar is yours," I say in a low voice.

Daniel's eyes narrow as he thinks about it, but Mom calls out, "Didi, don't do whatever your jiejie is telling you to do. I have more bars."

Foiled by Mom's superpowers again. I have no idea how she always knows what I'm up to, but Daniel's face is red with fury because I almost got him to take my dishwashing shift for a measly granola bar. So I'm going to call that a win.

Then Mom comes back from the garage and hands Daniel a box of bars. "We won't be able to get more unless they go on sale again," she says tiredly. "So don't eat them all at once." *Have those dark circles always been under her eyes?*

Dad comes over and puts a hand on Mom's shoulder, and she leans against him.

A strange tightness seizes my chest, and Daniel and I exchange glances. He stops trying to grab my hand, and I silently give him the granola bar. We know better than to fight when our parents are obviously struggling to hold it together. Mom and Dad aren't telling us how bad it is, but we can read between the lines.

Daniel and I might not always get along, but we do have one thing in common.

We'd do anything for our family.

I wish I knew what was bothering my parents. But I have the same queasy feeling I had at the center yesterday. *Something is wrong.*

SIX

TINA, MY CHINESE SCHOOL BEST friend, flops into the seat next to me in the back row and sighs in relief. "Only four mistakes this time."

"Nice going!" I say admiringly. "You just tied my personal best score!"

"I'm just happy if I stay under ten mistakes," she says modestly.

"I, on the other hand, am a fan of reasonable goals," I say, "so I'm shooting for between ten and fifteen. That's the sweet spot so a teacher won't expect too much of you, but won't think you're a complete loser either."

Tina's eyes crinkle, and I can tell she's trying not to crack up.

Auntie Li says Tina and I have *way* too much fun together at Chinese school, but she hasn't separated us yet. Tina and I, who are both twelve, are the oldest kids in the class. Most kids age out of Chinese school by now. Once kids get to middle school, they can make their escape with the usual excuse of needing extra time to study for "regular" school. Since my parents own Hong Chinese Academy, that's not an option for me, and Tina stays because I'm still here.

It would be cool to have a Chinese friend at Clarktown Middle School. Of course I love Lauren and Kelli and would go to the ends of the earth for either of them, but sometimes I wish Tina were my regular-school friend too. Unfortunately, she goes to middle school in a different town, so instead, I have thorn-in-my-side Max as a sworn enemy.

Auntie Li calls up Daniel to turn in his homework, and Tina whispers to me, "Seriously, how do you think you did?"

"Not great." My gut twinges with anxiety. "Let's just say it's a good thing you didn't need all the pennies I gave you." Maybe I shouldn't have tried to do my homework while marathoning *Never Have I Ever* last night. Technically, I wasn't allowed to watch it. Mom says twelve is too young for a show with such "mature" language and content, which just made me want to watch it even *more*. So, after finally figuring out how to get around the firewalls of my school-issued laptop (which is supposed to be strictly for homework)—I couldn't resist starting the show. I swear I was going to watch just one episode before doing my homework, but . . .

"Ah," Tina says sympathetically. She opens her mouth like she's about to say something else, but Auntie Li has finished her correction of Daniel's homework in what might be record time, and she's looking around the room for her next victim. Silently, Tina slips me the remainder of the pennies I had given her.

Smoothly, I drop them into my pocket just as Daniel reaches his desk in the front row (where he always sits). He twists around in his seat to give me a hard stare. He must suspect that I've been sharing my pennies.

I stick out my tongue at him, but unfortunately, this catches Auntie Li's attention. Oops.

"Hong Li Hua," she says sharply. "Come up and hand in your homework." Yup. Auntie Li is in full-on laoshi mode.

Reluctantly, I walk up the aisle to Auntie Li's desk, the pennies jangling in my pocket with every step. I absolutely hate turning in my homework right after Daniel.

Auntie Li's mouth sets as I hand in the sheet of graphing paper with my wobbly-looking characters crammed into the blue squares. With an air of resignation, she uncaps her red pen and pulls my homework toward her, across the desk.

Nervously, I shift from foot to foot, and each little *scritch* of her pen makes my heart quake. Wow, that's a lot of red.

Finally, she's done. Auntie Li jams the cap back on her pen and drops it onto her desk, where it rolls around aimlessly. Even the pen looks disappointed in me. "Er shi ba," she says stiffly.

Twenty-eight? That can't be right. Before today, my worst score was fourteen. This is double that. Then I look down and count up all the missed dashes. For one character, I had gotten halfway through . . . and just forgotten to write the rest. My teacher had generously marked that as one mistake. Oh. There are twenty-eight mistakes, all right.

Well, it's not like anyone can flunk out of Hong Chinese Academy. More than one kid has tried, thinking they can stop coming if they do badly enough.

No one's ever succeeded.

With a mental shrug, I pull out my bag of pennies, and Auntie Li's gaze bores into me as I start counting. "Yi, er, san . . ." Each time I count out a penny, I set it carefully on the desk, and when I'm finally finished, there's a gleaming pile of pennies on the scarred wooden surface. I grab my homework off her desk and turn to go, but she stops me.

"Li Hua, wait. Your mother showed me your semester report card." Auntie Li says this in Mandarin with a sprinkling of English. Outside of school, it's just the opposite—mostly English with a little Mandarin. "You got straight As. Congratulations."

I'm not sure what I was expecting her to say—but it

wasn't that. "Xiexie?" At least I remember to thank her in Mandarin even if my voice lifts at the end like I'm not sure what I'm thanking her for.

But she's not done. "So I know you can do better *here*."

My cheeks go scalding hot, and I don't know what to say. I'm not used to being tongue-tied. Then anger flickers in me. The deal I made with my parents is that they won't pressure me about Chinese school as long as I attend regularly and do all my homework. And I've kept my end of the bargain—more or less.

Auntie Li must sense my defiant thoughts because her eyes narrow. "That Zhang boy does well in *both* American and Chinese school."

Oh, no she didn't. The thin paper of my homework begins to disintegrate in my hot, sweaty grip. This is way worse than being compared to Daniel. Wild horses couldn't drag this from me—but deep down inside, I'm proud of my little brother. Somehow, he manages to be his gloriously geeky self *and* popular at school. Still, even he comes in second to Max—already a legend in our small Clarktown Chinese community even though he's only been here two years. Academically gifted. Speaks fluent Mandarin. Sickeningly polite to adults (although he's never said a nice word to *me* in his entire life). But I know his secret. "Max Zhang is a total jerk!" I blurt out.

"Zhen de?" a smug voice from behind me says in flawless Chinese.

Chills crawl up my spine. *It can't be.* But as I slowly turn around . . . I already know who I'm going to see.

Max Zhang.

My stomach drops about a mile. "Yes. Zhen de," I say. And because I can't say it with enough sarcasm in Chinese, I repeat it in English. "Yes. *Really.* A total jerk."

Auntie Li gasps. "Lily! How can you be so rude to our guest? Apologize at once!"

"Sorry," I mutter.

"No problem," Max says, so politely that it makes me want to throw up. But I'm not fooled. I see the spark in his eyes. For him, getting me in trouble is probably better than a dozen birthday presents plus cake and ice cream. It's a good thing he didn't get here in time to see me shell out all those pennies.

But what is he doing here? He goes to that fancy-schmancy Chinese school in the city! It's bad enough that he showed up at the theater yesterday, but it's totally unfair that he's at my Saturday Chinese school too. Is he *trying* to ruin my life?

Auntie Li finally sends me back to my seat and introduces Max by his Chinese name, Min Zhe. Then she tells the rest of the class that he's here to visit for the day to see if he'd like to attend Hong Chinese Academy.

I'm not buying it. There's something else going on.

And I know what it is.

Max has obviously decided to take our feud to the

next level—by coming onto my turf. And the worst part? I can't win against him here at Chinese school. I mean, I just made twenty-eight mistakes on my homework.

Frustrated, I throw myself into my chair.

"What's wrong?" Tina whispers.

"That," I say in a voice full of doom, "is Max Zhang."

"Oh." Her eyes go round. She's heard me complain about him before.

Auntie Li finishes her introduction. Then Max takes the floor and gives us a speech *in Chinese* about how glad he is to be here . . . blah, blah, blah.

Honestly, I don't understand half of what he's saying, but judging from Auntie Li's misty-eyed expression, Max must be sucking up hard.

But the awe on Auntie Li's face is nothing compared to the dopey way Daniel is leaning forward in his seat like he's trying to get closer to his new idol. You'd think he'd be mad about being knocked off his star-student pedestal. But no. After Max is done, my little brother actually claps. Traitor.

I glare at Max as he takes the seat next to mine.

"Cheer up, Lily," he says with a grin. "This is going to be fun."

I'd tell him exactly how *not* fun this is for me if Auntie Li weren't watching me with eagle eyes.

Then she claps her hands for attention. "Our new student isn't the only surprise today!" she tells the class.

"Principal Hong is going to make an announcement in a few minutes."

What announcement is this, and why didn't Mom tell me about it?!

Right on cue, my mother walks into the room with her best "I'm professional and approachable" principal smile.

"Do you know what's going on?" Tina whispers to me.

"Not a clue," I whisper back grimly. This had better not be another scheme like the pennies to "prove the value of our school."

My mother avoids my eyes as she faces the class. *Not a good sign.* "Good morning," she says. "I am here to tell you about an exciting opportunity. The Clarktown Community Center is having its first showcase!" The fluorescent lights flicker overhead, giving her words an unintended creepiness.

We all look at each other in confusion. Okay, that's seriously weird. We barely have working lights, and the community center is putting on a show? Tina nudges me, and that's when I realize that all eyes are all on *me*, like the other students are expecting me to get to the bottom of this. *Well, I can try.*

My hand shoots up, but I'm talking even before she calls on me. "Why now? I mean, is there a reason the center is doing a show?"

"We just felt it was the right time." Her smile looks

like it's been glued in place.

"Is this a contest like the school Clarktown's Got Talent video competition?" I ask. What's going to happen when it comes down to a choice between eliminating a senior Zumba act and a preschooler act?

"No, no." She shakes her head. "It's not a competition at all. It's a showcase of all the wonderful things happening at the community center, which is why the students of Hong Chinese Academy will be performing as a group."

Over. My. Dead. Body. This is *worse* than the penny punishment. Way worse. I do *not* want to be reciting the sayings of Confucius in Chinese or something equally cringey with the whole town watching.

"Traditional Chinese dance!" Mom continues. "You'll be the hit of the show."

Okay . . . I hit pause on my protests. This might not be quite as bad as I thought it would be. "Who's going to be teaching us how to dance?"

"I am," she says cheerfully as she passes out permission forms.

Mom knows Chinese dance? This is news to me.

"*You're* going to teach us?" Daniel asks.

I guess Mom's secret life as a dancer took him by surprise too.

"Yes, Daniel. That's what I said," she says, sounding a little offended.

My little brother shrugs. He probably would have

preferred reciting dead Chinese philosophers, but he's generally happy to roll with almost anything.

I glance at Max, surprised he hasn't said anything snarky yet, but he's got a weird blank look on his face. Chinese dance must seem like the seventh circle of hellish geekdom for a cool kid like him. The thought cheers me right up.

"Participation is optional, but this is a wonderful opportunity," Mom says.

That's when the permission slips reach my row. Tina hands me the last one, and I start reading. *Rehearsals will take place after school Monday through Friday at the Clarktown Community Center.*

My heart goes cold. Oh no.

All around me, there are groans.

"You've got to be kidding!"

"What? Another hour of Chinese school!"

I barely hear the mutters around me. In total shock, I'm staring down at the paper.

Rehearsals are from 4:00 to 5:00.

With the time it takes to walk from the theater to the center, the dance lessons will cut into our measly hour of film rehearsals by *ten minutes*. Definitely scratch the part where I thought my mom's plan wasn't so bad. My hand shoots into the air, but Mom ignores me.

"Emails with more details have been sent to your parents." That's code for *Participation isn't really optional. If your parents sign you up, then you're going to be putting on a sparkly headdress and spending every afternoon learning Chinese dance.* Then she looks right at me. "Rehearsals start a week from this Monday, and permission forms are due by next Saturday. Again, this is a wonderful opportunity."

Yeah, my permission form is definitely already signed and filed. My stomach starts to fill with dread.

Kelli and Lauren are counting on me. It was already going to be hard enough to win the Clarktown's Got Talent video competition (and making history as the first middle school winners) with only an hour of rehearsal time. Now their director has to duck out of rehearsals ten minutes early? The dread in my stomach gets bigger. What am I going to tell them?

SEVEN

THE LONGEST DAY I'VE EVER experienced of Chinese school is finally over—and I still haven't figured out what to do.

"Bye, Jiejie," Daniel yells as he sprints toward Dad's classroom. I'd go with him and try to get Dad to change Mom's mind about afternoon dance lessons except I know there's zero chance of Dad overruling Mom.

"Dance lessons could be fun!" Tina says as we leave class. "We'll get to hang out every day!"

"Uh, yeah," I say as I hustle her up the stairs, hoping to avoid Max.

Her face falls at my less-than-enthusiastic response, and guilt stabs me. I try again. "Dance will definitely be cool." Of course I want to see more of Tina. Just not at the same time I'm supposed to be with my *other* best friends.

Max bounds up the steps and catches up to us. "Hi," he says to Tina, "I think Lily forgot to introduce us. I'm Max."

She gulps. Obviously, she knows he's supposed to be Enemy Number One, but it goes against her nature to be rude. "Uh, hi." She glances at me nervously.

"Max, this is Tina. Tina, this is Max," I say rapidly. "He's. The. Worst," I stage-whisper, still pulling her up the stairs.

"Ha! You should talk! Look closely during the next full moon," he advises Tina, "and you'll see her forked tail."

"Full moons are for *werewolves*! How do you not know that?"

"Nerd!" He's grinning.

"Can't you think of a better insult?" I ask coldly.

"Well, 'the worst' was already taken. And 'jerk' too, apparently."

Tina's eyes dart between us like she's a rabbit trapped by two predators. Lauren and Kelli might be used to me fighting with Max, but this is all new to her.

When we reach the top of the stairs, I grab Tina's hand and practically race down the halls to the front doors. The good news is that we leave Max in the dust. The bad news is that we almost run right into my mom and Ms. Zhang.

"Buyao pao!" *No running.* Mom holds out a hand to stop us, but we've already come to a screeching halt.

"Duibuqi," Tina and I both apologize breathlessly. Mom is definitely going to lecture me later about running down the halls in front of Ms. Zhang.

Ms. Zhang is wearing a posh all-white pantsuit and pointy heels. Her hair is chic and layered, and her makeup has that barely there look that's in all of Kelli's fashion magazines. *Who dresses like that to pick up their kid from Chinese school?* "Ah, so nice to see you again, Lily," she says in English.

Mom's lips press together. She clearly doesn't like Ms. Zhang speaking to me in English as if I don't understand Chinese, but Mom just switches to English and says, "This is Tina Wang. She also attends Hong Academy."

"Nice to meet you, Tina," Ms. Zhang says.

Max strolls up to us. "See, Lily," he says, "that's how you introduce people."

His mother's forehead wrinkles. "What are you talking about, Max?"

He's not going to rat me out, is he?

Because she knows me too well, my mother glares at me suspiciously. She's just going to *love* hearing that I called Max "the worst."

My skin goes clammy. There aren't any rules in this war of ours—but we've never tattled on each other before.

Max glances at me and then looks away. "Nothing," he mutters.

Whew. Who knew he had a tiny bit of decency after all?

"So, Max," my mother says, "what do you think of our school?"

Here's another chance to throw me under the bus, but he just smiles without looking at me. "It's nice."

"Thank you so much for letting him visit!" Ms. Zhang says. "He kept asking—"

"Ma!" Max's face reddens.

I knew it! This was all Max's idea. He just couldn't pass up an opportunity to torment me.

My mother's voice loses a bit of its stiffness. "Then you will consider enrolling Max in our school?"

"Ah. That is . . ." Ms. Zhang's face turns as red as Max's. "I think maybe I wasn't clear. This is just a visit for Max. We couldn't possibly take him out of his other Chinese school. The academic focus there is so good. You understand, don't you?"

"Of course." A fake smile that looks like a thin slash forms on Mom's face.

Anger burns in my stomach. The last thing I wanted was for Max to come to our school, but that doesn't mean his mother gets to make snobby comments about us.

Max looks down at his feet, and if I didn't know better, I'd say he looked almost disappointed. But of course that's ridiculous. Why would he want to go to a school with burned-out light bulbs?

In fact, his mother is looking around now, her glance seeming to linger on the faded carpet in the hallway and the cracked paint on the walls. "It's such a shame." She puts a hand on my mother's arm. "What are you going to do, Xiaozhang?"

Usually, Mom loves being called "Principal" in Chinese, but apparently *not* by Ms. Zhang. From the strained look Mom gives the perfectly manicured hand on her sleeve, you'd think a cockroach had just landed on her. "What do you mean?"

"Oh, you know." Ms. Zhang's sympathetic smile slips, and she quickly lifts her hand from my mom's arm. "I hear that the owners can't afford to keep the community center open. That means you'll have to find a new location for your school, doesn't it?"

What?! The blood rushes to my head, and I actually feel dizzy with shock. "Mom, is this true? Are Ms. Moreno and Ms. Leticia going to shut down the center?"

Tina gasps, and we clutch each other's hands for support.

Max takes a step back from me like he thinks I'm going to hit him or something. *I just might.* Even if this isn't, technically, his fault.

"There's nothing to worry about, Lily," Mom says, but a muscle in her cheek twitches. "The Morenos are just a little behind in their mortgage, but we're all working on a solution."

So that's why Ms. Leticia, Ms. Carter, and Mom were all meeting yesterday! And that's why Mom and Dad have been so stressed lately. My throat tightens.

"I'm so sorry!" Ms. Zhang says, eyes wide. "I didn't know it was supposed to be a secret that the center is in trouble."

"Thank you for your concern," Mom says, "but the center will be fine. Janet and Sam Carter are working with us and the Morenos to turn the center into a non-profit."

I let out a breath I didn't know I was holding. All I know about nonprofits is from Lauren, but she talks about them like they're the answer to everything—plus rainbows and chocolate sprinkles. So maybe everything will be okay.

"It's . . . a lovely idea," Ms. Zhang says hesitantly. "I'm assuming your nonprofit will be taking out a loan to buy out the balance of the Morenos' mortgage?"

"That's the plan," Mom replies coldly.

"I see. I hope it works out. Banks are being conservative in their loans these days." She pauses and lowers her voice. "If I can give you some advice, Sara, from one business-woman to another—a center that needs so much work is a risky investment. If you can't get enough of a loan, I would strongly recommend that you *not* use your own money."

Loan? Our own money? I mean, Mom is rationing granola bars. No way do we have any money to help buy the community center. My body starts to shake. If the center closes, our school will have nowhere to go.

"Of course not," Mom says, her back straightening. "Besides, it won't be necessary. The bank has already pre-approved a loan for the Clarktown Community Center Nonprofit, and our showcase will bring in enough to cover what the loan doesn't." Her jaw firms. "Clarktown Community Center's first-ever showcase is sure to be a successful fundraiser."

Mom didn't say anything before about the show being a fundraiser. My stomach turns wobbly and sour.

"Oh. A showcase." Ms. Zhang smiles politely, but condescending pity practically oozes from her voice. "Yes, I got your email. So you will be teaching the children traditional Chinese dance?"

My mom's eyes flash dangerously. *Uh-oh.* I know that look. That's exactly how she looked last year when a new mechanic tried to overcharge her. At first, she had kept her calm even when he talked too loud and too slowly to her, but then he said, "That's just how we do things, here in America. It's not like wherever you come from." She made Daniel and me leave with her right then and there. Without our car. Dad had to pick it up later.

My mom is usually a calm and rational person, but sometimes her pride gets the better of her. And then all bets are off.

Now Mom pulls herself up to her full height and says

in a ringing voice, "Actually, I won't be teaching the children. I have someone else in mind."

Um. What? Who's going to be teaching us?

"I'm inviting a professional dancer to teach the children. She used to dance for the Fenghuang Performers. Of course, you've heard of *them*."

I've never heard of the Fenghuang Performers, but from the instant lift of Ms. Zhang's eyebrows, it looks like she has.

"The phoenix dance group?" Max asks.

I jump a little to hear him speak. For once, I had forgotten he was there. Of course "Mr. Speaks Perfect Chinese" knows what *fenghuang* means. *I* only know what *fenghuang* means because my favorite Chinese fairy tale is about a phoenix.

"We saw them once," he says. "Remember, Mom?"

"Yes, I remember. They were amazing." She turns to my mother. "How did you find a dancer from the Fenghuang Performers to teach here?"

"She's an old . . . friend of mine."

Whoa. Mom is full of surprises today. Why hasn't Mom ever mentioned her famous dancer friend before?

"What's her name?" Ms. Zhang's voice sounds just a touch impressed.

My mother's face freezes for a second. Then she takes a deep breath like she's about to jump off a high cliff.

"Vivienne Hou."

EIGHT

"*VIVIENNE HOU?*" AUNTIE LI SCREECHES. "Are you out of your mind?"

Daniel shoves me in an effort to get closer to the door but I don't budge. I've never once heard a fight between Mom and Auntie Li, and I'm not about to give up my prime spot with my ear plastered to the classroom door.

"If you don't stop shoving," I hiss, "they'll figure out we're listening and then we'll never find out who Vivienne Hou is."

Daniel grunts in resignation and squats down in the hallway to take up a lower position.

Dad is speaking now. "I don't know what you two have against Vivienne."

"Nothing," Mom and Auntie Li chime together. There's a pause, and I can imagine them exchanging a meaningful look.

"I don't have anything against her," my mother says.

"Me neither," Auntie Li says too quickly. "I just don't understand why you're changing the plan, Sara. I thought you were going to teach the kids."

"Ellen, I took dance classes years ago when I was just a kid in China. The parents won't be impressed by that. Elizabeth Zhang certainly wasn't. But you should have seen her face when I said Vivienne would be teaching our students."

"So all of this is just so you can impress Elizabeth Zhang?" Auntie Li asks stiffly.

"Of course not." Mom sighs. "But she was right when she said the banks are being conservative. The Morenos want to sell to our nonprofit, but they also need to clear their debts. A successful fundraiser is the only way we can raise enough money to buy the community center. And if people hear that Vivienne Hou is training our students to perform in the show . . ." Her voice trails off hopefully.

"How much does the fundraiser need to make?" Dad asks.

There's a long pause before Mom finally says, "A hundred thousand."

A hundred thousand?!

Daniel gasps, and we look at each other with wide eyes. That's a lot of money. And except for the Zhangs, the people of Clarktown aren't exactly known for their wealth.

"There's got to be another way." Auntie Li sounds

desperate. She must really not like this Vivienne Hou.

"There isn't another way." My mom sounds determined. "I'm not going to let the Morenos go bankrupt *or* lose our school."

My heart thuds to my feet. I don't want those things to happen either. So, if I have to take dance lessons to save the community center and our school, then that's exactly what I'll do.

Auntie Li doesn't respond. Instead, it's my father who says, "Vivienne might be classically trained in Chinese dance, but how are we going to afford to pay her enough to come back to Clarktown and teach our students?"

So Vivienne Hou is from Clarktown. *The plot thickens.*

"I hear she's living in New York and between jobs," Auntie Li says reluctantly. "She might be available." Her voice goes sharp. "For a *short-term* job."

"Just until the showcase is over," Mom agrees.

"Do you really think she'll come back to Clarktown?" Dad asks.

"She will," Mom says grimly.

Vivienne Hou sweeps into the community center auditorium ahead of my mother and Auntie Li. She's carrying a huge tote bag and wearing flowy black pants, a bright red top that matches the shade of her lipstick, and dangly silver earrings that peek out beneath her sharp, sleek bob of black hair. "Children!" she proclaims, climbing the steps to the stage and setting her bag on the floor. "I'm delighted to meet you!" She actually does seem happy as she examines the nine of us who have signed up for lessons.

As for me—I'm about as far from happy as you can get. In fact, my stomach is a tangled mass of guilt, and my knees are shaking like a bowl full of iced jelly. All because I just lied to Lauren and Kelli about having a dentist appointment to get here on time. *What was I thinking?* There's no excuse for lying to my two best friends. I'm going to have to confess. *Tomorrow*, I promise myself.

Daniel is looking back at Vivienne with an eager expression on his face, but I frown in suspicion. No adult can possibly be this thrilled about teaching a bunch of kids forced to be here by their parents. What kind of favor did Mom call in, anyway?

Mom and Auntie Li don't come onto the stage. Mom is smiling her fake smile, and Auntie Li isn't smiling at all. Her mouth is pressed together, and I can almost hear her grinding her teeth to powder. I've never seen either of them look so tense, but Ms. Hou doesn't seem to be feeling the tension at all. Her every movement crackles with energy as she smiles at us.

We all greet our new dance teacher. "Nihao, Laoshi." I probably sound the least enthusiastic.

Vivienne shudders. "No need to call me Laoshi."

Tina and I look at each and shrug. "Nihao, Teacher," we all chorus.

"No. No." She shakes her head so hard that her earrings swing wildly. "Call me Vivienne!"

Right. Like Mom will ever let us call an adult by just their first name.

"Well," Mom says brightly, "it looks like you've got things under control, so we'll be going now."

Auntie Li is already out the auditorium door and isn't looking back.

"Leaving already?" Vivienne's red lips form a perfect pout.

Mom looks after Auntie Li's retreating back. "I'll have you over for dinner soon," she says. "We can get caught up then." She hurries away, calling, "Ellen, wait up!"

Vivienne stares after them for a long moment before turning back to us. Then her eyes land on me, and her whole face lights up. "You," she announces, flinging a hand out to point at me dramatically, "are Lily Hong!"

My mouth drops. "H-how do you know that?" I stammer.

"Your hat, of course!"

I reach up to touch the soft wool of my favorite hat. The red one with pink roses from my anonymous fairy godmother. "You're the one who sends presents every Lunar New Year!"

Daniel bounces on his toes. "I love that cool model train you sent last year!"

"Ah, you must be Daniel!"

I'm still reeling in shock that she's our secret gift-giver. So . . . Vivienne isn't just someone who owes our mother a favor. In fact, they must be pretty close for her to send us awesome stuff every year. But why hasn't Mom ever mentioned her before?

Vivienne beams at us. "You like my presents? Your mom always says you do in her thank-you cards."

I wince. Mom doesn't send thank-you cards to people she likes. She calls or sends a text or maybe even an email. A formal card is the kiss of death for Mom, but I can't tell Vivienne that. Luckily, I really do love the presents she gave me. "Yes," I say. "The book of Chinese myths you gave me is great!"

"I knew you'd like that book," she says in satisfaction. "Which story is your favorite?" Normally, an adult who asks what my favorite anything is doesn't really care about the answer, but Vivienne actually looks like she wants to know.

Maybe that's why I tell her the truth. "Actually, my favorite story isn't in the book." My favorite story is the one my dad used to tell me every night when I was little, a story from the Hui Chinese Muslim—my people. "It's the one about the phoenix who turns her body into the city she loves so she can protect it."

"Ah! 'The Phoenix and Her City.'"

"You've heard of it?" I ask in surprise. I've never seen the story in any book, and I've actually suspected that my dad made it up, especially since he keeps changing the details of the story, like having the messenger goose deliver Girl Scout Cookies to the phoenix. Somehow, I don't think that was in the original.

I want to ask Vivienne how she knows about the story, but she's already snapping her fingers, saying, "Look at the time! We had better get started. Boys to the right and girls to the left, please!"

Yikes. This is exactly how the square-dancing unit in fourth-grade PE (a.k.a. every kid's worst nightmare) started. Is Vivienne going to make us hold hands until our skin goes slippery with sweat as we stumble around, stepping on each other's toes? It's going to be hard to partner us up since there are only two boys.

She tells the boys, "You are going to be lion dancers!"

Daniel and Louis high-five each other, and Vivienne makes Daniel (who is a year older and an inch taller) the head of the lion and assigns Louis the tail.

Lion dancers, huh? Maybe this won't be so bad. Our parents took us up to Vancouver, Canada, one year for the Lunar New Year parade, and I loved the acrobatics of the lion dancers who performed there.

"And you girls," she says, walking over to her big tote bag and opening it up, "are going to be fan dancers!"

On the other side of the stage, Daniel doubles up with laughter. "Oh boy! I'm glad we get to be lion dancers!"

Secretly, I agree with him, but I glower at him on principle. "Oh, shut up!" Envy burns through me like acid. I wish I could trade places with Daniel. It would be so cool to be a lion dancer.

The other girls start chattering excitedly.

"Do we get to wear costumes?"

"This is so awesome!"

Vivienne smiles and pulls a fan that must be about two feet long out of her tote bag. Then, with a graceful flick of her wrist—she opens it, and white feathers tipped with a wide stripe of bright pink spread out in a smooth arc.

The girls all crowd around Vivienne, and Daniel abruptly stops laughing. In fact, he's staring at the fan with an odd expression on his face, and if I didn't know better, I'd think he was actually *jealous*.

"Can I hold it?" one of the girls asks.

"It's beautiful!"

Even Tina gets in on the action, pulling me along with her in her enthusiasm.

Smiling, Vivienne starts handing out fans and presses one into my reluctant hands.

The white wooden handle feels slick and unnatural in my grasp. "Why can't *we* be lion dancers?" I demand.

"Trust me—you're going to love this, Lily!" She snaps her fan closed. "Okay, girls, line up by height, please. Tallest here by me."

Still skeptical, I go stand next to Vivienne. The next girl in line is Julia, who's in fifth grade and a year younger than me, then Tina, then Mia, who's in fourth grade, then Audrey and Rose, who are both third graders, and finally Kylie, a second grader.

"Good. Good." Vivienne goes down the line, nodding like she's a drill sergeant inspecting the new recruits. Then she comes back to me. "Lily, you're the tallest, so you're our lead dancer."

Julia, who's barely an inch shorter, glares at me. "Why does she get to be the leader just because she's a little taller?"

"Julia can lead us," I say at once. If fourth-grade square dancing was any indication, I am in no way qualified to be the lead dancer.

"Oh no, it would ruin the symmetry!" Ignoring Julia's mutters, Vivienne spreads open her fan, tosses it so it does a neat midair flip, catches it one-handed, and snaps it shut in a seemingly effortless sequence of movements. "Now let's practice!"

Okay, I admit it—the way she handles that fan makes her look like one of those butt-kicking women warriors in a Chinese wuxia drama. I can *totally* see her wielding her fan as a kung fu weapon, blocking sword thrusts and sending her opponents sprawling with one well-timed flutter of her fan.

No wonder Daniel keeps sneaking glances over to our side of the stage.

Then Vivienne leaves us to practice tossing and catching our fans while she goes to work with the boys, and I discover the new bane of my existence. Fans.

It just slips through my fingers when I try to catch it. The other girls seem to be struggling just as much except for Tina, who's actually catching her fan almost every time.

Frustrated, I throw my fan too high in the air, and it wobbles off to my right. "I got it!" I yell to no one in particular, like I'm a wide receiver in a football game.

"Hey, watch it!" Julia yells.

But it's too late. I crash right into her as the fan escapes my outstretched fingers once again, and then, from my dazed position on the ground, I watch it all happen in open-mouthed horror.

Julia tumbles to the ground, catching Tina's elbow on the way down so that Tina falls too, fumbling her fan and accidentally whacking Mia in the head with it. On her way down, Mia stumbles into Audrey, who tries and fails to regain her footing by grabbing onto Rose, who falls on top of Kylie.

Cringing, I look at the girls around me, sprawled out on the stage among white and pink feathers. It's like we're in some bizarre circus clown/bird comedy act.

Vivienne comes running over. "What in the world happened?"

I think Julia is going to make some snide comment about me as the lead dancer, but she just stands up, dusts herself off, and stretches out a hand to help me to my feet. "It's harder than it looks," she explains calmly. Then she goes back to tossing her fan in the air.

I've always liked that girl. Like any family, the students at Hong Chinese Academy don't always get along, but we've got each other's backs.

The rest of the girls groan and slowly stumble to their feet—except for Kylie, who bounces up and says, "That was fun!"

Vivienne sighs. "Well, I was going to work next on doing a flip with your fans, but maybe we should just focus on catching them. Without falling down."

She probably regrets leaving her glamorous life in New York and coming here to work with a bunch of klutzes.

The only thing that cheers me up is that Daniel, for once, isn't doing any better. Instead of practicing the steps that the lion dancers are supposed to do in sync, my brother is yelling at Louis, who keeps trying to leap onto Daniel's back. I guess Louis is trying to imitate the lion dancers he's seen—despite Vivienne's attempt to explain that those kinds of moves are too advanced for them, and anyway, it's the *tail* dancer who holds up the head. . . .

No wonder Daniel didn't cackle at the sight of us going down like a row of dominoes. He's got his own problems.

"No, no! Stop!" Vivienne calls out as Louis takes a runner's starting position and launches himself at Daniel, who's practicing a bunch of crouched, side-to-side steps that makes him look like a crab.

Daniel looks over his shoulder, straightens abruptly, and scoots out of his path. But Louis keeps coming, and within seconds, their "practice" has turned into Louis chasing Daniel around the room, trying to leap onto his back.

"Stop!" Vivienne waves her hands (somehow managing to look graceful) as she runs to intercept the boys.

I catch Tina's eye, and she bursts into giggles. Daniel dodges around *both* Louis and Vivienne, and my own laughter bubbles up—only to be cut off suddenly by an unwelcome sight.

Max Zhang is staring at us through the open doors of the auditorium.

NINE

MAX HAS A RAPT EXPRESSION on his face as he watches Vivienne chasing after the boys.

Anger rises in me. *How dare he sneer at us in all his snobby uber-coolness.* This time Max can't claim to be just walking by.

I stalk across the stage, trying to snap my fan shut like Vivienne does, but it stays stubbornly open, so I have to stop and fold it up—which does *not* have the dramatic effect I was going for.

Gripping my fan, I hurtle down the steps and up a side aisle. I'm seriously over him stalking my every move. It's time to have it out with Max.

I'm almost to the doors when he finally notices me and goes pale.

I storm right up to him. "Ha! I caught you this time!" I'm so angry that I wouldn't be surprised if actual smoke were coming from my ears. "Admit it!" I level my fan at him. "You're spying on me so you can tell everyone at school that I'm a dork who does traditional Chinese dance and then make fun of me for it."

"No! I wouldn't do that." He throws up his hands. "I think it's cool that you're working with Vivienne Hou!"

I eye his hands to see if he's got a phone out to record me failing at fan-tossing practice. There's no phone, but there *is* a crumpled-up piece of paper in one fist. A shiny piece of paper that's red and black. "Hang on," I say slowly. I've seen that paper before . . . outside the school theater and hanging on the community center bulletin board. "Is that the flyer for a new dance club?"

He instantly puts his hands behind his back, and his face reddens.

"It is!" My eyes widen. What are the chances that there would suddenly be a dance audition at the school theater *and* a new dance club at the community center? All the pieces start falling together. That day Max was at the theater, he must have been holding auditions for a dance video. I'll bet no one showed up, and if he's anything at all like me, he'd move to Plan B. And that would mean . . . "*You're* the one who's trying to start a dance club at the community center?" I don't believe it. Too-cool Max is the last person I would have suspected, especially since it looks like his Plan B worked just as well as Plan A—which is not at all. Unexpected sympathy twinges in me.

"What's this?" Vivienne glides up to us. "Did you say this young man *dances*?" I can't tell if her breathy voice is from excitement or if she's just out of breath from chasing Daniel and Louis around the stage. "What's your name?"

"Max Zhang." He takes a step backward. "And uh, I don't have any actual training."

Vivienne's eyes are bright and she doesn't seem to be listening. She grabs him by the arm and practically drags him into the auditorium. "You must join us!"

"He doesn't even go to our Chinese school!" I protest, following them back onto the stage, where everyone stares at us with open curiosity.

"Oh, that doesn't matter," she says airily.

Mom might say otherwise, but I'm not about to tell her about this, so I try another strategy. "You don't even know if he can dance!" I turn to Max. "Can you?"

He glances around the stage, where everyone is quiet and leaning forward to hear his response. "I guess," he mumbles, "but not the kind of dancing you do, Ms. Hou."

"Call me Vivienne!" she says promptly. Then a smile of delight spreads over her face. "You knew my name! Have you heard of me?"

The red in his face deepens to brick as he nods and stares at a spot on the wall. "I've seen you perform." He looks at me nervously, like he fully expects me to make fun of him for being a fanboy.

But I'm speechless. Is this really Max, blushing and shy around my dance teacher?

"You see!" Vivienne turns to me. "He has a *passion* for dance. I can tell these things."

What she means is that she's so desperate for decent dancers that she's going to recruit any Chinese kid who walks by and happens to be a big fan of hers, and who's trying (unsuccessfully) to start a dance club. . . . *Okay, fine!* I guess I can see why Vivienne would think that Max is the answer to her prayers.

"Have you ever done lion dancing?" she asks him.

He shakes his head, but his eyes light up. "No, but I've watched a bunch of YouTube videos."

"Good. Just a moment!" She pulls out her phone and a Bluetooth speaker from her tote bag and cues up music with the beat of drums and clashing cymbals. "Show me."

Oh, this should be good. No way is "Mr. Too Good for Ordinary Mortals" going to bust out his lion-dancing moves in front of all of us.

But that's *exactly* what he does.

Before I know it, Max is leaping in the air and coming back to earth in time to the crash of cymbals. He starts popping and locking in a way that I've never seen in a lion dance—but it's seriously amazing. He's even doing that fancy side-stepping thing Daniel was trying to do—only he makes it look cool, like he's harnessing all the ancient spirits plus a couple of TikTok stars in his twelve-year-old body.

In other words, Max Zhang is a *scarily* good dancer.

Everyone else seems to think so too. When the music ends and Max comes to a panting stop, all the kids start clapping and cheering. And are those tears glistening in Vivienne's eyes? "That was magnificent!" she exclaims.

Normally, the sight of Max being praised by a teacher and all my classmates applauding him would be the stuff of nightmares. But the fundraiser has to be a success to save the community center. . . .

Max catches my eye and goes very still. It's like he's holding his breath and waiting for me to make fun of him for being a geek who's *obviously* practiced all those YouTube moves in his room.

But I just don't have the heart. Vivienne is right—Max clearly has a passion for dance. Keeping my gaze locked on him, I say, "I guess we've got a new dancer."

He gulps and looks like he's going to say something, but then Daniel breaks in with excited questions. "How did you learn how to do that? Can you show me?"

Tina nudges me. "I thought you'd be more upset about this," she whispers. "I mean, is he still The Worst?"

I shrug. "Maybe, but anything to give the show a boost, right?"

She grins. "Right."

"Daniel," Vivienne declares, "you and Louis will trade

dancing as the tail of the lion. Max, you will be the head of the lion!"

This gets better and better. Now I can make fun of Daniel for being the butt of the lion.

"Cool!" Daniel elbows Louis. "No more trying to jump on my back!"

"Actually," Max says, "I don't mind being the tail if you two want me to lift you up as the head. Not on my back though." He smiles and bends his knees so his thighs form an angled platform. "Want to try?"

"Sure," Daniel says happily.

To my surprise, Louis shakes his head. "Uh, no thanks. I'm good." It looks like he was more interested in messing with Daniel than actually trying out lion-dance moves.

There's no way *I'd* refuse. It's not fair that my little brother gets to do cool acrobatics while I'm stuck with the fans.

"I'll leave you boys to it, then," Vivienne says. "Girls, back to work!"

I groan. I had forgotten that Max joining us means that he's going to see me crash and burn at dancing. Glumly, I follow the others back to our side of the stage to start the mind-numbingly boring routine of throwing and catching my fan again. I look over my shoulder to see Daniel wobble and fall off his perch on Max's thighs. The sight cheers me up immediately. I bet I wouldn't fall off. I might fumble my fan nine times out of ten, but I *am* good at balancing.

With a sigh, I toss my fan in the air and barely manage to grab it before it hits the ground, but only by cheating and using both hands. I sneak a glance at Max to see if he noticed, but he's too involved with taking Daniel and Louis through dance steps to pay any attention to me.

Toss, fumble, drop. Toss, fumble, catch. Toss, drop. Over and over again, I practice until my arms are numb and my fingers feel about as coordinated as overcooked spaghetti.

"Can I give you a tip?" Max says from right next to me.

I'm so startled that I jump about a mile in the air and drop my fan. "Look what you made me do!" It's totally unfair because chances were that I was going to drop it anyway.

"Sorry," he says easily, like I hadn't just snapped at him for no good reason.

I look around. The other girls are still practicing, but after I caused that domino-effect fall, we've all spread out to give each other space. Daniel and Louis are gamely practicing their steps, although they're still not even close to being in sync. Vivienne is nowhere in sight. "Where's Vivienne?" I ask.

"She went to go get something."

"Oh." I don't know what to say to Max if it's not something snarky. This might be the first time we've had a conversation where we're not fighting.

"About the fan," he says. "I think you're trying too hard and getting too stressed. If you keep your eye on the fan, your hand will automatically follow, and I bet you'll catch it a lot more."

It can't be that easy. Can it? "I guess it's worth a try."

He gives me an encouraging nod, and my palms prickle with sweat to have him so near and watching me probably drop the fan again.

Actually, I'm used to him waiting for me to mess up. What I'm *not* used to is him rooting for me, and that makes me so nervous that my heart is pounding overtime.

I take a deep breath, heft the open fan a few times, and then I toss it in the air. White and pink feathers fill the edges of my vision, but I keep my eyes glued on the painted wooden handle. My hand shoots out . . . and I'm holding the fan. "I did it!" I turn to Max in excitement, forgetting that he's my enemy.

"That's awesome!"

For a beat, we just stand there, grinning at each other.

Then Vivienne's voice breaks the moment. "Gather around, everyone!" She climbs the steps back up the stage. "I have something to show you!"

I tear my eyes from Max and go with the others to where Vivienne is standing with a sheet of paper in her hand. It's the order of performances for the showcase, and ours is listed as the last one.

"This is such an honor," she says. "The Hong Chinese

Academy Dancers will be headlining!"

I don't have the heart to tell her that performing last isn't exactly headlining. Last year, the Quilting Club had a quilt-a-thon in the auditorium with my dad as the last "performer," and no one thought that *he* was the headliner. In fact, most people were asleep by the time Dad took the stage for his shift.

Vivienne is still waving the list of acts around. "With us getting the top billing, the fundraiser is sure to do well. And that's especially important with the news your mother got today."

Um. What news?

"Wow!" Max says over brightly. "We'd better practice hard, then!"

I give him a hard stare. I know a desperate bid for distraction when I see it, but what is he trying to hide?

"What news did my mom get?" I ask Vivienne, watching Max's eyes go wide and panicked.

Her expressive face goes serious. "The owners are going to sell the community center to someone else if the nonprofit can't make enough money from the fundraiser to buy it themselves."

"Someone else?" I say disbelievingly. "Who?"

"I have no idea." She claps her hands together. "Good work today, children. Tomorrow, we'll start learning steps. This dance will be the best thing Clarktown has ever seen!"

My eyes fly to Max's pale face, and my mind races. Max is being weirdly nervous. The Morenos might have to sell the center. Max's parents are developers. Hot anger sweeps through me. Vivienne might not know who is trying to buy the center, but I do.

Max's family.

TEN

WHEN I GET TO SCHOOL the next morning, I don't go to the library to meet Kelli and Lauren like I usually do. Instead, I lurk impatiently at the back entrance. Yesterday, Max bolted right after Vivienne dropped the bombshell about the community center, so I wasn't able to confront him right then and there, but he won't be able to avoid me at school.

Luckily, I don't have too long to wait before a sleek silver Tesla pulls up to the curb and Max jumps out.

The car barely has time to pull away before I run over and plant myself in front of Max. "I knew you were being way too nice!" I yell, making other kids turn and stare at us. "You've been coming to the center to spy for your parents. First Chinese school and then the dance rehearsals!"

"You've got it all wrong!" He glances around and

waves at a couple of other kids, like he's saying, *Hey, nothing to see here. Just Lily going all ballistic for no reason.*

But I *do* have a reason. "Your parents are trying to buy the community center out from under us, but they won't succeed! The Morenos won't sell to them. They're going to sell it to our nonprofit."

"That would be fine if your nonprofit had enough money to buy the center," he says, adjusting his slouchy beanie, "but it doesn't."

I want to knock that hipster hat off his head or at least mess up the slouch he probably spent hours in front of the mirror getting just right. "Don't pretend with me. I know what's really going on." I remember Ms. Zhang looking down her nose at the peeling paint and old carpet when she picked up Max. "Your parents think they can just swoop in like vultures and take our center away from us."

"You don't know what you're talking about." His voice rises with anger. "My parents just want to help!"

"How is *this* helping?"

"Look," he says, voice dropping, "what do you think will happen if your nonprofit can't come up with the money to buy the center? The bank will foreclose on the Morenos, then they won't get anything, and your Chinese school won't have a home."

He has a point. My body turns cold at the thought of the bank taking the center.

"My parents could get the center for a lot cheaper if they buy it from the bank," he continues, "but this way, the money will go to the Morenos."

The hot anger rushing through my body cools a bit. Could he be telling the truth? Maybe I've been jumping to conclusions. "What about Hong Chinese Academy?"

"My parents don't want to see your school close down either," he says, taking a step toward me. "They'll figure out a way for you to keep it."

I'm starting to waver. Did I misjudge Max and his family? Then again, isn't it a little weird that Max is so eager to join our amateur Chinese dance troupe? If his parents send him to Chinese school in Seattle an hour away, why aren't they getting him professional dance lessons there? *The rat.* Max wasn't spying on me—he was spying on the center for his parents.

That's when I hear Kelli's voice. "Lily! Where have you been?"

I turn to see Kelli and Lauren coming through the school doors. They clearly got tired of waiting and came looking for me. Without stopping to think, I burst out, "Max's family is buying the community center!"

Lauren and Kelli just stare at me blankly.

Don't they get it? My hands bunch up into tight fists, and my eyes narrow on Max suspiciously. If his parents buy the center, what's to stop them from making it into something much fancier and hiking the rent way up?

"They're going to ruin the center!" My chest is tight with fury. "No one will be able to afford it. The preschool, the clubs, our school—we'll all be kicked out!"

Lauren gasps, and Kelli gives Max a look that she usually reserves for fashion disasters, but I'm pretty sure there's nothing in Max's designer jeans and Converse high tops that could offend her stylish sensibilities.

"That's awful!" Lauren says. *Her* tone is the one she usually reserves for big businesses exploiting . . . yeah, there's no mystery about why she's upset.

Max is starting to back away from us, but I'm not going to let him go that easily. "How did your parents find out about the Morenos' money problems, anyway?" I ask, my tone dripping with hostility. "And what exactly are your parents planning to do with the center?"

"I don't know!" he says. "But I'm sure it will be something great."

I snort in disbelief. "Yeah, right. Great at completely destroying it!"

Lauren's face shines with righteous indignation. "We'll fight you with our dying breath!"

Okay, I'm pretty sure that last part was a line from *The Chosen One Slays Big Business on the Hellmouth*. But except for the fight-to-the-death part, I agree completely with Lauren. "She's right," I say. "We won't let you take our center."

"It's not like we're *stealing* it!" His voice rises in

frustration. Then he looks around and says more quietly, "Listen, can we talk about this later? Everyone's looking at us."

He's right. People are used to me yelling at Max, but the three of us ganging up on him is making kids stop in their tracks, curious about what we're fighting about.

Max turns and quickly walks away, calling out to a friend of his. This time I let him go. Anyway, it's not like he can escape this. Hong Chinese Academy isn't the only organization dependent on the center. Half the town belonged to some club or took some class there at some point. When news of his involvement gets out, Max is going to become a social outcast. I almost feel sorry for him.

"He's not going to get away with it," Kelli says. Then she pulls out her phone.

My stomach sinks. "What are you doing?" She wouldn't, would she?

"Posting on Instagram about Max's parents taking over the community center," she says, like it should be obvious.

That's what I was afraid of. "Listen, Kelli," I say, dropping my voice down to a whisper, "I don't think it's a good idea to post about Max's parents buying the center."

"Why not?" Kelli demands so loudly that Max glances back at us. She takes the opportunity to snap a picture of him, and he frowns.

For some reason, I think back to second grade when a kid asked me if I ate dogs—and how horrible it made me feel. When I asked her why she would think that, she simply said, "Because you're Chinese."

I don't want these kids to think of Max in the same way—someone strange and foreign, but I don't know how to explain it to my friends. I struggle with a hard lump of words before turning to my friends and saying, "They'll look at Max like he's some crazy-rich Asian coming into town and taking over."

"But—" Kelli starts to say, but Lauren cuts her off.

"I get it." Her eyes are full of understanding. "I'll go and distract everyone from wondering why we were all yelling at Max." Lauren strides over to the other kids and says, "Let me tell you about the youth climate summit I'm organizing. . . ."

And she's off. If I know her, she'll have half the school making signs and volunteering for the youth climate summit by lunchtime.

Max is staring after Lauren anxiously and isn't even looking at me. He probably thinks Lauren is telling them about his parents.

Well, that's gratitude for you, but he doesn't know that I told my friends to keep quiet about his parents buying the center.

And that reminds me . . .

"I mean it," I say, turning to Kelli. "Not a word about

Max or his family."

Her eyes shift between me and Max, who's still looking at the crowd of kids surrounding Lauren. "Oh, you've got to be kidding me."

"What?" I ask in confusion.

Her mouth is starting to curve up in a smile. "You and Max, huh?"

In dawning horror, I realize the *epically* wrong conclusion she's come to. My whole face flames up. "Oh! No, it's not what you're thinking!"

"You have a—"

I pull her close to me by the sleeve of her pink leopard-print jacket. "I do not have a crush on Max," I hiss into her ear. "And if you even hint at such an awful thing again . . ." I trail off and let the implication of what I'll do hang threateningly in the air. Partly for dramatic effect. But mostly because I don't know what I'll do.

"Fine! Fine!" She bats my fingers away from the faux fur of her jacket. "I won't say a word about Max's parents to anyone else, but if you think you can keep me from talking to you about the *other* thing, then you don't know me at all."

I lunge for her, but she dances out of my way and goes to join Lauren, who may have just started a mini rally in the parking lot.

Defensively, I call out after her, "You're wrong!"

"Wrong about what?" Max asks, coming up to me.

He's clearly realized that Lauren's impromptu climate rally has nothing to do with him.

"You . . ." I sputter angrily, ". . . are nothing but trouble."

Then I spin around on my heel and stalk away from this whole mess that is absolutely, one hundred percent Max Zhang's fault.

ELEVEN

LAUREN IS LAUGHING SO HARD at lunch that her eyes are watery, and I'm afraid she's going to snort her milk out of her nostrils. "Lily likes Max? You're delusional, Kelli!"

"That's what *I* told her!" I glare at Kelli, my so-called friend. I couldn't stop her from sharing her ridiculous theory with Lauren, but that doesn't mean I can't defend myself. I mean, she made us sound like some kind of middle school Romeo and Juliet—and I don't even like Max *as a person*. NO WAY do I like him as a *crush*.

"I'm telling you," Kelli insists, "it totally makes sense! Why else would you be fighting from day one?"

"Because Max is a jerk—that's why!" I pound the plastic cafeteria table for emphasis, making all our lunch trays bounce dangerously. This has gone on long enough. It's time to get us back on track. "We have to find out what his parents are going to do with the center."

"But, Lily," Lauren says, wiping a stray tear of laughter from her cheek, "how do we even find out?"

I glare at her. This is the girl who made Kelli and me help her take water samples from the Clarktown River and then convinced our science teacher to help us analyze the samples to find out who the biggest polluter was. And now Lauren's asking me how we find out what Max's parents are going to do with the center? Yes, water pollution is bad, but isn't the fate of the community important too? My spine straightens. "For the past few days, Max has been coming onto *my* turf. It's time he got a taste of his own medicine."

Kelli's eyes widen. "What are you going to do? Show up at his Chinese school in Seattle?"

"No. I have a better idea." I stand and pick up my tray. "Girls," I say dramatically, "I'm about to crash *The. Table.*"

We all look over to the table in the cafeteria where the cool kids eat their lunches. Max, of course, is right in the center of all that oozing popularity. There's so much hip fashion and tech that it looks like a cutting-edge commercial set and not a real cafeteria lunch table. That's the table where the eighth-grade class president, the vice president, the basketball team captain, and the cheer squad captain sit. And then there's Max—a seventh-grade new kid who's somehow charmed his way into the middle school royal court.

"They'll eat you alive," Kelli says solemnly, turning back to me and running her eyes over my factory outlet jeans and *Buffy* fandom shirt.

"Besides," Lauren says, "I'm not sure you'll get any information by going over there."

"Then I'll settle for embarrassing him in front of his snobby friends." I grin. I can't wait to watch him squirm as he tries to explain away his uncool "friend" from the community center.

Lauren just shakes her head, but Kelli is bouncing up and down on the plastic bench of the cafeteria table. "Go for it, Lily!"

I start to raise a fist in a power move but almost drop my lunch tray, so I settle for giving a determined nod. "Wish me luck!"

Then, head held high, I march over to the enemy camp—a.k.a. the cool kids' table.

There are only five kids at their table. Max, two other boys, and two girls. One of the girls is showing the other one something on her phone, and they're saying things like "I can't believe she thought it was Insta-worthy. I would have never posted that!"

The two boys are across from each other, playing a game on a console, and they're saying things like "Dude, you just got me killed!"

Max has Beats headphones on and has his back to me, so he doesn't seem to notice as I approach.

But his friends do.

One of the girls says, "Um, what's this girl doing here? Does anyone know who she is?"

Your worst nightmare, I want to say. Except it might actually *be* her worst nightmare to have a geeky seventh grader approach her holy table. At least, that's the impression I'm getting from the look of disgust on her face.

The two boys look up from their game, and the one sitting next to Max nudges him. "Do you know this girl?"

Really? Just because we're both Asian—this guy assumes we know each other? But that *is* what I'm counting on. *Guilt by association, Max.* I bounce on my toes in anticipation. Maybe he'll try to pretend that he doesn't know me. Ooh, I can't wait to see him squirm.

Max takes off his headphones and turns around. His eyes lock on me, and he gives a little start of surprise.

Here it comes—sweet victory. I can almost taste it.

But then his face splits into a huge grin. "Lily! Come, sit down with us!"

My mouth drops open in shock. What the heck is going on? Why isn't he dying of humiliation from being associated with me?

"Brady, scoot down," he says.

Brady doesn't budge. Instead, he crosses his arms like he's daring me to make him move.

Max frowns but then pats the space on his other side. "Sit here, Lily."

Dazed, I plunk my tray on the table. *I guess I'm doing this.*

While Max introduces me to his friends (Maddy P., Maddy C., Brady, and Theo), I frantically run through the devastatingly snarky comments that I'd prepared on the way over here.

Too embarrassed to introduce me to your friends, Max? Except he's *literally* introducing me now.

I'd offer to share my tater tots, but your head would probably explode if you tasted the food of the commoners. But this new, eerily friendly Max would probably just share whatever is in that white cardboard box in front of him that practically screams "fancy catering service."

He's done with introductions and is looking at me expectantly, so I unlock my throat and say, "Hi." Not exactly the clever insult I had planned.

One of the Maddys (Maddy P., I think) says, "So, what brings *you* to our table?"

"And what's up with that girl holding a stick?" the other Maddy chimes in.

It takes me a second to understand that she means my *Buffy* shirt. "It's a stake."

She looks at me like I'm speaking an alien language.

I sigh. "You know, to stab vampires with and turn them into dust?" I mime staking a vampire through the heart.

"Why does a girl need to go around carrying a stake?" Brady asks snidely.

"Because she's a vampire slayer." Which is pretty obvious since it says "Buffy the Vampire Slayer" in bloodred right on my shirt.

Theo laughs. "That show is so corny. I mean, my *mom* watched it."

"I've never seen it," Max says, glaring at Theo. Then he turns to me and asks with genuine curiosity in his voice, "What's it about?"

It's about a girl turning a bunch of snobby kids into vampire dust at lunch. . . .

Maddy C. groans before I can finish coming up with the perfect put-down. "Oh no!" she says with a wrinkle of her nose. "Please don't encourage her to talk about some boring show no one wants to hear about."

Max's eyes narrow. "Don't worry. She's not staying."

Aha. Now he's showing his true colors. But there's a hollow feeling in the pit of my stomach. Being right about Max doesn't feel as satisfying as I thought it would. In fact, it feels pretty crummy.

Then he stands up. "Come on, Lily. Let's go eat lunch with *your* friends."

Huh? Max inviting me to sit down with his friends already had my head spinning, but abandoning his friends to eat lunch with mine? That's an alternate-reality level of strange.

"Seriously, Max?" Brady asks. "You're actually going to eat lunch with a bunch of nerdy seventh graders?"

"I *am* a seventh grader," he replies, "and I want to hear about this show Lily likes, so I guess that makes me a nerd too." He looks at me. "Coming?"

I slowly get to my feet, *sure* there's a catch. Am I being punked? But he's grabbing his white catered box off the table like he means it, so maybe this is really happening.

The two Maddys have already gone back to their Instagram trolling, and the other boys are picking up their game consoles. It's like Max and I don't even exist to them anymore.

I pick up my lunch of hamburger and tater tots (which are probably stone cold by now). "Uh, okay, follow me, then," I say to Max.

On our way to our table, I say, "Are your friends going to be mad at you?"

He shrugs. "Nah. They don't really care what I do." His eyes shift away from me. "They're just . . ."

I think of how he could finish that sentence: . . . *actually from another planet so they're having a hard time acting like realistic humans? . . . at such a level of coolness that being nice would literally make their heads explode?*

"Not really my friends," he mutters at last.

It's the last thing I expected him to say, and I almost drop my tray.

He flushes. "What I mean is that they're not like your friends. Anyway, they won't give me a hard time. Tomorrow, it will be like nothing happened."

What kind of friends *are* these? If I ever left Lauren and Kelli to eat lunch with another group (except for emergency spy missions like this one)—they'd never forgive me.

Actually, judging from my friends' open mouths and shocked expressions as they watch us approach, I'm not entirely sure they'll forgive me for *this*. Right. I was supposed to go over there to get information—not invite the enemy to eat lunch with us.

"Listen," I say to Max in a low voice, "there's no time to explain, but can you not mention Vivienne's dance rehearsals to my friends?" I still haven't told Lauren and Kelli about Chinese school dance practice, and I really don't want them to hear about it from Max of all people.

"Why not?" His face wrinkles in confusion.

"Shh," I say frantically as we near the table where my friends are.

"Fine," he whispers, "but you're going to have to explain why later."

"That's fair." I'm not looking forward to that explanation, but I've got bigger problems right now.

"Hello," Kelli says coldly as we reach the table. She's looking at me in shock, and that's when I realize she never really believed her own hackneyed theory about my crush on Max.

Lauren doesn't say anything, but the way she rakes Max over from his slouchy beanie to his pristine Nikes makes her opinion of him clear.

"Max is eating lunch with us," I say in a small voice, taking a seat across from Kelli and Lauren.

"Hi," he says, sitting next to me. "Anyone want some dumplings?" He opens up the white container, clearly deciding to ignore my friends' subarctic vibes. "This place makes the best ones."

"Not possible," I say loyally. "My parents make the best jiaozi!" But the smell of chives, ginger, and spice-scented oil wafting from the open container is making my mouth water.

He grins. "Okay, these are the best *restaurant* jiaozi, then."

"No, thank you," Lauren says stiffly while Kelli shakes her head. They both stare at me like they're expecting me to refuse too.

And I know I *should*. But if Snow White's stepmother wanted to poison me, she wouldn't tempt me with an apple. She'd bring me a basket of jiaozi. The kind that's thick and doughy with the filling so juicy that it leaks a little out of the puckered folds at the top—which is exactly the kind that Max is holding out to me.

"No, I'm good," I say faintly, picking up a sad, soggy tater tot from my lunch tray instead. It is both too raw and overdone at the same time. My taste buds scream at me in protest. *You could have had delicious, flavorful jiaozi, and instead you're giving us fried reconstituted powder?!*

"Suit yourself." He pops a jiaozi into his mouth, and from the way he chews it with his eyes half-lidded in enjoyment, I can tell it's just as good as I had imagined.

A little part of me dies inside.

"So," Lauren says loudly, "let's talk about my role as the community organizer who's trying to stop big business from taking over Clarktown."

"Sunnydale," I correct her.

"Oops. Isn't that what I said?"

Kelli's eyes gleam. "Yeah. And we should talk about *my* slayer character's motivation for taking down the demon businessman. I think he should be really, really annoying."

"Sorry," Max says, "what are we talking about?"

"Our film," I say, stomach churning with anxiety.

"And Lily totally did *not* base the demon businessman on you," Kelli says, looking at Max.

The churning of my stomach becomes a full-blown tornado. *Don't say it, don't say it . . .*

Lauren looks like she might regret going down this path, but Kelli forges on. "The fact that our villain is named Maxistopheles Maxiavelli is just a coincidence."

"Oh. Okay." Max eats another jiaozi without looking at me. This time, he doesn't offer to share.

I shift uncomfortably in my seat, but I don't know what to say. Lauren and Kelli are now talking about math class and pointedly ignoring Max. *Great.* My friends are mad because *I* got them all riled up about Max's parents buying the community center and now he's eating lunch with us. Max is hurt because I wrote a villainous character who's (loosely) based on him. And why do I even care about his feelings, anyway? The heaviness in my heart when I look at Max's bowed head makes no sense at all, but in silent penance, I eat another gross tater tot.

This has got to be the most awkward lunch ever.

TWELVE

"OKAY, THAT DIDN'T GO AS planned," I admit to Lauren and Kelli after school as we're walking to the theater for the last rehearsal before starting the filming tomorrow. "But don't worry! I have a Plan B!"

Lauren stops in her tracks. "Maybe it's time to let this go, Lily. Max is never going to tell you what his parents are going to do with the community center."

"Besides, what are you going to do this time?" Kelli rolls her eyes. "Invite Max over to watch a movie with us?"

"No, Ms. Sarcastic." I try to roll my eyes too, but Kelli has kind of mastered the art, and no one can outdo her. "It's time to up the stakes. I'm going to invade Max's home turf. Literally." Dramatically, I fling my arm out to point across the street at the wrought iron gates of the Palisades.

"You can't be serious." Kelli's mouth hangs open in shock.

"Don't even think about sneaking into the Palisades!" Lauren grabs me by the shoulder and pulls me toward her, like I'm about to take off across the street without warning and start scaling the hedges or something. "It's gated for a reason."

"How are you going to even get in there?" Kelli asks.

"Simple." I pry Lauren's fingers from my jacket. "There's a gap between the gate and the hedge. I'll just squeeze through."

"And if you get caught trespassing?" Lauren demands. "Then what?"

"And what about rehearsals?" Kelli looks over to the theater, which is just a few blocks from the entrance of the Palisades. "If you get arrested, we lose our director and screenwriter!"

Lauren's eye roll isn't quite as good as Kelli's, but it gets her point across. "Kelli, your priorities are out of whack."

"I'm not going to get arrested!" But my heart *does* beat a little faster. I can actually imagine one of the snobby Palisades residents calling the police on a kid who looks like she doesn't belong there. "It's not like I'm going to break into Max's house. I just want to get an idea of what the Zhangs are going to do with the center. So I need to get a peek at the neighborhood they developed."

"But what about rehearsals?" Kelli looks defensively at Lauren. "It's a fair question! Lily had to leave early yesterday for a dentist appointment, and Lincoln totally tried to take over as soon as she left!"

Guilt twinges in me. I had almost forgotten about that little lie about the dentist *and* about my double life as the director of our film and reluctant fan dancer in the fundraiser performance. I was going to tell my friends everything today, but now I'm not so sure. Sure, the dance performance is for the center's fundraiser, but my friends don't have the same investment in the center that I do (despite the impressive coldness they showed Max at lunch). Besides, this video competition means so much to all of us, and I don't want Lauren and Kelli to worry about my attention being split.

"Are you okay, Lily?" Lauren is peering at me closely.

I've got this. It's only one more month of juggling two different but equally important parts of my life. And my stomach isn't hurting at all. That's just my imagination. "Sure! I'm fine. Never better." Wow, that was worse acting than I did as the Tin Girl in *The Wizard of Clarktown*.

Lauren looks doubtful, and Kelli's eyes narrow in suspicion.

"What's this about Lincoln causing trouble?" I ask in an attempt to change the subject.

"We handled him just fine," Lauren says calmly, "but Kelli does have a point. Why do you need to sneak into the Palisades right now?"

Um, because it would give me an excuse to get out of the last day of film rehearsal and make it to Chinese dance lessons on time? No, that's not fair to my friends. "You're right," I say. "I don't need to do this now. I'll go after rehearsal." I don't add that I plan to go after *dance* rehearsal.

Kelli's gaze turns from suspicious to thoughtful. "You know, I've always wanted to know what the Palisades looks like. I'll go with you."

"No!" I'm already regretting not telling them about Chinese dance, but I can't let them find out now after I lied about it. Kelli's eyebrows rise, and I add hastily, "I mean, uh, it will be better if I go on my own. With two of us, people might think we're, um, a girl gang or something. . . ." My voice trails off. *Come on, Lily, you've got to do better than that.* No one would mistake us for a girl gang.

"I guess you're right," Kelli says regretfully.

Really? She bought that?

"There's no talking you out of it, is there?" Lauren asks.

"Nope," I say cheerfully.

Lauren sighs. "You've got my mom's number in your phone in case you need a lawyer, right? Remember that you have the right to a phone call."

"And don't forget to check out the clubhouse," Kelli

adds. "It's supposed to have a heated pool!"

I straighten my spine. "Don't worry. This time, it will all go according to plan."

The first hitch to my plan comes at dance rehearsal.

Vivienne is *not* happy that I'm ten minutes late, but fortunately, she's not a yeller. She just sighs dramatically and tells me that she hopes I've been practicing with my fan at home because today, we're working with *two* fans and starting to learn steps, and the other girls have already gotten a head start. . . .

I think I would have preferred it if she yelled, but being late and dealing with Vivienne isn't really a setback.

That would be the sight of Max spinning and leaping while Daniel cheers him on. Why is he still here?! Isn't his secret mission for his parents over? He's already told them that the center is in trouble and that the Morenos might have to sell it. What else does he hope to find out?

Max catches sight of me midspin and stops to wave at me.

Nope. He doesn't get to pretend that we're suddenly buddies. Besides, he's just being nice to cover up his spying. I cross my arms without waving back, and his face goes all pinched.

An uncomfortable feeling creeps over me. I mean, he *did* stand up to his horrible friends for me. And I don't really believe that he's just here to stab me in the back again. I mean, no one can fake this kind of joy in lion dancing.

Vivienne's eyes drift to the auditorium doors, and I turn to see what's caught her attention, but I don't see anything. She seems distracted as she hands me two fans and moves away, saying, "Carry on! I'll be right back."

When I look at Max again, his back is to me, and he's saying something to Daniel.

Daniel glances at me and races over. He barely brakes to a stop before saying in a singsong voice, "Ooh, you're in trouble! Wait until Mom and Dad find out you were late to class!"

Luckily, I know how to handle my little brother. "I will make your life miserable if you snitch on me." My method is pretty simple actually. Start with a threat. End with a bribe. "One day of dishes." It's a lowball offer, but we both know Daniel isn't a tattletale.

The bribe isn't to keep him from telling on me. It's to stop him from bugging me about being late . . . because this won't be the first time. Yes, we start filming at the center tomorrow, which will cut down on the commute from the school theater. On the other hand, there's no high school musical limiting the time we have to film at the center. *Wow. I really did not think this through.* My mouth goes dry, and the month leading up to the showcase suddenly seems like an eternity.

"A week of dishwashing," Daniel counters.

"No way. Three days. Final offer."

"Deal." He sticks out his hand, and I shake it.

Then I look over to where Max is all by himself, leaping so high in the air that it looks like his Nikes are jet-powered. "You'd better get back to practice. Where's Louis, anyway?"

"He decided he wanted to be a part of his class video for the Clarktown's Got Talent competition, so he talked his parents into letting him quit dance."

"What is his class doing for their video?" I ask, trying to play it cool.

He doesn't fall for it. "Even if I knew, I couldn't tell you."

Well, it was worth a shot. It's part of the competition to try to find out what the other entries are, not that anyone tries very hard to find out what the middle school videos are going to be. All attention is on the high school and elementary school.

"Wait a minute!" A sudden realization fills me with unholy glee. "If Louis is out, that means you have to be the lion's butt!"

Daniel doesn't seem fazed. "It's the tail, actually. And I get to hang out with Max. He's really cool!"

"You do know his parents are trying to buy the center, right?"

He shrugs. "Someone has to buy it."

Before I can explain about big developers and remind

him of the nonprofit Mom and the Carters want to start, Tina comes over.

"Three days of dishes," Daniel reminds me before rejoining Max.

"Is everything okay?" Tina asks. "Why are you late?" For all my faults at Chinese school, being late isn't usual for me.

"I just got busy after school," I say vaguely.

She hands me two fans. "With your other friends?" There's no judgment in her voice, but my Spidey-sense tingles anyway.

"Uh, yeah." My face goes hot. Technically I *was* hanging out with Lauren and Kelli, but that's not the whole truth, and I know it. Maybe I should tell her about the film, but I'm already picking up weird vibes in the way she said "other friends," and I don't want to make it worse. Besides, she doesn't go to middle school with me, so she doesn't get why the video competition is so important. I swallow to wet my suddenly dry throat. "Two fans, huh? Sounds hard."

"It's a little tricky, but I'll show you." She flicks both fans open and holds one up in the air and one down by her waist. Then she switches the position of the fans. "We're supposed to practice doing this."

That seems easy enough, but when I try it, a fan catches in my hair on the way down. I bet Max would have some helpful tip like: *Try putting your hair in a ponytail.* Or some snarky comment like: *It's a fan, not a hat.*

But Max seems to be ignoring me, and he's doing a better job of it than I am because I keep sneaking glances to see if he's looking at me. He's not.

Frustrated, I say, "This is it? We just move the fans up and down? I thought Vivienne said we'd finally practice steps today."

"We are, but she said we couldn't start without our lead dancer."

Right. That's me. I hunch my shoulders and gracelessly flip-flop my fans like a chicken trying to fly.

Tina presses her lips together as if she's trying not to laugh. Then she models the moves again, looking like some kind of fairy with pink-and-white wings.

"You know, you're really good at this!" I say with genuine admiration.

"Thanks!" She grins at me. "Do you want to stay after for a bit to practice? My mom can't pick me up until later anyway. After we practice, we could go to Ice Yum Palace and get some ice cream."

"Oh." My mind races through excuses. But I come up empty, so I blurt out, "I can't. I have to sneak into the Palisades after class to spy on Max." Wow. It really does *not* sound good when I say it out loud.

"Fine," Tina says coldly. "You could have just said you had plans with your other friends and are too busy to hang out with me."

My stomach lurches. "But I'm telling the truth!" My voice rises. "I really am—" I cut myself off because Max has turned to look at me, and I'm not about to announce my plans to him.

Tina shoots me a disbelieving look and walks away.

I've got to explain. But just as I'm about to go after Tina, my attention is caught by a glimpse of Auntie Li with Vivienne right outside the auditorium. Then Auntie Li suddenly hurries away without coming inside to say hello or even wave to me.

Vivienne sweeps back into the auditorium. "Girls," she barks in a very un-Vivienne-like way, "let's learn some steps." There's a hard glitter to her eyes, and her mouth is a tight line.

Automatically, I turn to tell Tina what I just saw, but she's whispering in Julia's ear, and the two of them are giggling with their heads pressed together. Something hard squeezes my heart.

All the girls line up, and it takes me a second to realize that Vivienne is back onstage and tapping her foot and waiting for me to take my place at the head of the line. As I hurry over, I catch a glimpse of Daniel making an awkward leap into the air.

"You've almost got it, Daniel!" Max says. "That was way better!"

Daniel pumps a fist in the air, and they high-five.

That figures. My little brother has been bewitched by

the enemy, my Chinese school best friend is mad at me, and my regular school friends are going to be irritated when I ditch out early from rehearsals *and* filming.

This is, somehow, all Max's fault.

As if he's pulled by the magnet of my rage, his head slowly swivels toward me, and our eyes lock.

I'm coming for you, I say silently in my head. It's payback time.

THIRTEEN

I REALLY DID NOT THINK this through. Twigs and prickly leaves poke at me as I squeeze myself between the hedge and the metal gate. Halfway through, my backpack gets stuck on something, and I have to shimmy out of the straps, disentangle it from the hedge, and then heave it onto the sidewalk. A minute later, I emerge from the hedge, panting and sweating with little bits of shrubbery stuck to my hot skin and tangled hair.

Then the gate slowly starts to open, and I grab my backpack and look for somewhere to take cover, but the only option is the hedge I just fought my way through. Going back into the hedge is definitely not an option.

So, I'm standing there on the sidewalk, clutching my backpack, and looking like a girl raised by wolves—as a Mercedes rolls through the gate. The car slows as the driver, a middle-aged white lady, stares at me.

My heart thunders frantically, but the Mercedes rolls on and out of sight as my pulse returns to semi-normal. That was close. Then I really take in where I am, and my jaw drops. Everywhere I look are huge houses with stone pillars and bright green manicured lawns. The sidewalk I'm standing on is so clean and white that you could easily eat off it. Even the *air* seems fresher than in the outside world. Maybe it's because of the trees lining the sidewalks or the landscaped medians in the streets.

Honestly? It's a little creepy.

I look around, and seeing no one near me, I take out my tablet and start taking pictures of the McMansions. If this is what the Zhangs have in store for the community center, then none of us will be able to afford rent in it. And I haven't even seen the clubhouse yet.

Stomach knotted with dread, I walk down the sidewalk until I spot a gleaming metal and glass building in the distance. Lifting my tablet, I zoom in and then squint at the screen. Is that a swimming pool enclosed in a glass dome? And that clubhouse must be at least four stories tall. I snap a picture, but I need to move in closer to get a better shot. . . .

"Lily Hong!" a voice exclaims.

My blood curdling in fear, I turn slowly to find that I'm standing right in front of the tallest mansion with the most sleek and modern wood-and-glass architecture. It can only be the Zhangs' house. And the fact that Ms.

Zhang is standing in the doorway is kind of a giveaway. *I am in so much trouble.* She is going to be furious that I've snuck into the Palisades to spy on them.

Except she doesn't look mad at all. She's beaming as she rushes down about a million steps and crosses about an acre of yard on a cobbled path to get to me. Maybe that's just how rich people act when they're about to go ballistic on twelve-year-old kids.

I should run, but I'm frozen in sheer terror. Sweat is making my armpits sticky, and I'm so light-headed I think I'm going to pass out. What if she tells my mom what I've been up to? I texted my parents to tell them I was doing homework with Lauren and Kelli, so on top of everything else, they'll be mad that I lied to them.

"Lily, what a wonderful surprise! Are you here to see Max?"

"Uh . . ."

Without waiting for an answer, she practically drags me with her down the path toward their mansion. "He's not home yet."

That's weird. I took my time dropping Daniel off at Minecraft Club so Max had plenty of time to get home before I even stepped foot in the Palisades.

"He'll be back soon," Ms. Zhang says, "and he will be so happy to see you!"

Wanna bet? But this is better than her thinking I'm trespassing, so I just smile through gritted teeth and let her usher me up the natural wood steps and through the double doors into a light-filled room, where I take off my shoes.

Ms. Zhang presses a button on the wall, and a whole panel of the wall slides open to reveal shelves and shelves of shoes. Seriously, what kind of people have a secret wall of shoes in their house?

Without even blinking at my worn and scuffed sneakers, Ms. Zhang picks them up and places them on a low shelf right next to a row of gleaming brand-name shoes that must belong to Max. Then she hands me a pair of red embroidered slippers from a different row.

Weird. My mom has the *exact* same pair of slippers that she keeps near the entrance for guests. Somehow, this detail is way more surprising than anything else in this multimillion-dollar home.

But that's where the similarities end because Mom keeps the guest slippers in a hall closet crammed with winter coats and sports equipment—and not on a dedicated shelf behind an automated wall. We also don't have an entryway sunroom big enough to fit our entire kitchen into, and our shoes at home are heaped into a messy pile on a tray by the door.

Ms. Zhang scoops up something from the floor and hands it to me. "Is this yours, Lily?"

"Oh yeah. Thank you." I take the green gem on a silver chain from her and fasten it back around my neck.

"I'm always losing Anyanka's amulet."

"I'm sorry?" she asks politely, a tiny crease on her forehead.

"Anyanka is a demon on the TV show *Buffy the Vampire Slayer*, or at least she was before she lost her powers and became Anya. . . ." *Stop talking, Lily! She doesn't care about the details of Anya's redemption story.*

"How interesting!" Ms. Zhang seems super determined to be nice. She leads me through the house, chattering a hundred miles a minute. "Max never invites anyone over. I was starting to think that he didn't have any friends at all!" She pauses at that like she's waiting for an answer.

I snap my jaw closed and tear my eyes away from a room filled with vintage arcade games. "Oh, he definitely has friends at school." Mean, snotty ones that I wouldn't wish on my worst enemy . . . which, come to think of it—is Max.

"Yes." She smiles at me like I'm an unexpected present wrapped in a *Buffy the Vampire Slayer* T-shirt. "I can see that he *does* have friends." She pulls me into a granite-tiled kitchen with every high-tech gadget in the universe. "Are you hungry?" Without waiting for an answer, she waves me to a seat and strides toward a refrigerator with blinking lights and a screen set into it.

"No, I'm fine," I say. "Thank you."

But she's already opening the shiny silver door of her

refrigerator and taking out a tub of hummus, a bag of carrots, some kind of pale cheese, a bottle of lemonade, some strawberries, and—from the freezer—a bag of frozen dumplings, edamame, and a box of mini quiches. It's like she's been preparing all her life for the sudden appearance of a twelve-year-old kid at her house.

She pours me a glass of lemonade and *talks* to the refrigerator, telling it to pour ice cubes for the lemonade. No wonder building a robot Minotaur for an extra-credit video wasn't such a big deal for Max. Then she rinses the strawberries, arranging them, the cheese, and the carrots on square white plates and sets them in front of me with the tub of hummus. "I'll heat up the things from the freezer, but first, let's see what else I have."

"This is plenty," I protest, feeling trapped and desperate. Am I really supposed to eat all of this?

She ignores me . . . as I knew she would. An eerie feeling of recognition is starting to creep over me as she runs to the pantry and magically pulls out a box of chocolate chip cookies, individually wrapped pineapple cakes, shrimp chips, pita chips, blue corn tortilla chips, crackers, wasabi peas, cashews, a loaf of bread, and a bar of dark chocolate. Arms full, she teeters a bit as she unloads the food in front of me like an overly generous genie.

There's a reason this seems all so familiar, and it's because . . . this is what *my* mother would do.

Mom's eased up over the years, but the first time Tina

or Lauren or Kelli came over to my house, it was exactly like this. Half the cupboard and refrigerator emptied to feed my friends.

"Try the pineapple cakes," Ms. Zhang urges. "They're not the kind you get in the stores here. I brought these back from Taiwan recently."

My mouth waters. I've only had pineapple cakes directly from Taiwan one time, but they've had a starring role in my dreams ever since. "Oh, thank you!"

Ms. Zhang goes to heat up the dumplings, edamame, and quiches, and I unwrap the thick waxed pink paper from the pineapple cakes reverently.

One crumbly sweet bite in, and I'm in heaven. These are even *better* than I remembered. Then a wave of confusion crests over me. The Zhangs are the ones trying to buy the community center and stop the center from becoming a nonprofit, but how can a woman who gives me pineapple cakes and reminds me of my mother be all bad?

I've just crammed the last bite of pineapple cake in my mouth and am wondering what I should start on next when I'm interrupted by Max's stunned voice from the entrance of the kitchen.

"Lily, what are you doing here?!"

"Isn't this a nice surprise?" his mother chirps from the stove, where she's frying up dumplings. "Lily came by to see you!"

"She did, huh?" His eyes are narrowed with suspicion.

I can't say I blame him. I mean, I'd feel the same way if he suddenly showed up in *my* kitchen.

"How was Chinese school?" his mother asks, putting a lid over the pan.

Shock courses through my body. Max hasn't told his parents that he's doing dance rehearsal with Vivienne after school? *And* he's skipping Chinese school to do dance?

A panicked expression flits over his face, and he gulps. "Um, it was good." His eyes swivel to me. "Lily, can I talk to you?"

"Why don't you and Lily go into the dining room?" his mother suggests. "And take the snacks with you! I'll bring the rest when it's done cooking."

Max and I gather up what we can and bring it to a long room with a heavy-looking dark wood dining table that looks like it could seat twenty. There's some kind of twisty, colorful glass sculpture as the centerpiece on the table, and the chair cushions are covered in embroidered black silk. Overhead, a legit chandelier glitters and sends sparkly light into the room.

Max drops his load with an audible thump onto the table, and shrimp chips go flying. "Okay, what's the *real* reason you're here? Is this your idea of revenge or something?"

He's got me there. I did come here to spy on his

neighborhood to see what the Zhangs had in store for the community center. Except I wasn't expecting his mom to invite me into their house. "Not exactly," I mumble.

"Well, now that you're here, go ahead—make fun of me and my family! I bet you're dying to make a judgy comment about the wall of shoes or the arcade or the sauna or the video-editing studio—"

"You have a *video-editing studio*?"

He glares at me. "That's not the point."

"Okay, let's put a pin in the video-editing studio." *We're totally going to revisit that topic.* "I'm not here to make fun of you."

"That would be a first." Then his eyes shift away, and his shoulders drop. "You're going to tell my mom that I'm doing dance instead of going to Chinese school." He doesn't say it like a question. I have him backed into a corner—and he knows it.

I've just been given a hunk of kryptonite. I mean, you'd have to set aside the whole "Max is Superman and I'm Lex Luthor" implication to make that metaphor work, but the important thing is that I finally have a way to beat Max.

There's only one problem.

I can't do it. After all, Max kept my secret about dance from Lauren and Kelli when I asked him to. The weird thing is that I don't think he'd tell them even if I rat him out to his mother. "Don't worry," I say. "I won't say a word about dance."

Relief sweeps over his face. "Really?"

"Yes," I say firmly. For the first time in days, it feels like the weight on my shoulders has lifted a bit. "But seriously, how do your parents not know that you're skipping out on Chinese school in Seattle?"

He shrugs. "My driver takes me to wherever I need to be, and my parents are too busy to check up on me."

Oh. My heart twists at the casual way he said "my parents are too busy." Darn. Now I can't even mock him for having a driver.

His mother appears at that moment, holding a huge tray of food and wearing an even bigger smile. A delicious smell of garlic and sweet chili wafts into the room. "Anyone hungry?" She starts setting the food on the table, and Max shoots me an anxious look behind her back.

I roll my eyes at him. What does he think I'm going to do—tattle on him after I promised I wouldn't? *Please.* "This looks delicious," I say happily.

FOURTEEN

"PLACES, EVERYONE!" I CALL OUT, resisting the impulse to glance over my shoulder. *Relax, Lily.* No one meets in this part of the community center except the Fencing Team, so it's not as risky as it might seem to shoot our film in the one building where Mom spends most of her time. And it's not like I'm actually trying to keep the film secret. For one thing, I had to get permission from Ms. Moreno to film here. I just don't want Mom to know what's making me miss so much dance rehearsal . . . or the fact that I *am* missing dance rehearsal.

At one end of the hallway, Kelli, as the slayer, swings a fake axe in one hand and Lincoln, as her ordinary friend, lifts his plastic stake. Behind them, Lauren (as the slayer's mentor) and Marissa (as the slayer's witch best friend) huddle over an encyclopedia bedazzled to look like a spell book.

At the other end of the hallway, Tim (as the demon businessman) and Suzie and Chelsea (as vampire minions) are looking appropriately menacing in full flaky gray makeup. "We're ready," Suzie says, sounding impressively clear for someone with vampire fangs in her mouth.

I look over the actors. "Kelli, hold your axe with both hands," I say. "No, not like you're going to chop wood. Remember that it's a heavy, wicked weapon that you're wielding—not a plastic prop."

"Got it." She adjusts her grip.

"Good." I nod in satisfaction. "Now, Lincoln, take a couple of steps back. Kelli is the slayer with super-strength and healing abilities. You want to help her, but you know you're an ordinary guy who can get hurt."

Lincoln grimaces but does as I ask.

Whatever. As long as Lincoln keeps his ego in check long enough to take my directions, he can sulk as much as he wants. "Now, Lauren and Marissa—"

I'm interrupted by a door opening. Glenn from the Fencing Team pokes their head out. "Hey, Lauren. What's going on?" Back when Glenn was in sixth grade and Lauren was in fifth grade, they were in crosswalk patrol together. Now Glenn is an eighth grader and the youngest member of the community center Fencing Team.

Lauren almost drops the spell book prop, but luckily,

Marissa catches it. "Hi, Glenn!" Lauren says in a breathless, very un-Lauren way. "We're just filming a movie."

Huh. It's not like Lauren to get flustered. This is the girl who bandaged up Kelli and me with Band-Aids she kept in her Hello Kitty purse whenever we scraped our knees. Hands down, Lauren is the first person I'd want in an emergency because she *never* loses her cool. Not that you'd know it from looking at her now, blushing and starry-eyed . . .

My breath catches. *Oh!* So that's why Lauren was acting super weird when I suggested doing our filming outside the Fencing Team practice room.

"Really?" Glenn's face lights up. "What's it about?"

"It's about a slayer going up against a demon businessman." Lauren's voice has almost returned to its usual calm, but she can't seem to meet Glenn's eyes.

"Lauren plays the activist mentor," Kelli and I say at the same time. We glance knowingly at each other.

"She's amazing in the role," I say.

"The best!" Kelli says enthusiastically.

Lauren shoots us a glare that clearly says, *Stop being so obvious.* "They're exaggerating."

"It sounds pretty awesome to me." Glenn comes all the way into the hallway, and the rest of the Fencing Team crowds in behind them. "Can we stay and watch?"

"Of course," Lauren says before I can answer. She hasn't looked this happy since her petition forced

Clarktown Hospital to dispose their waste in a more environmentally friendly way.

I bite down on about a dozen reasons why the Fencing Team shouldn't stay. "Fine, but no talking and no interruptions. We're on a tight schedule." I sneak a glance at the time display on my tablet. *Gulp.* I have to get to dance rehearsal in half an hour.

"You have to pick up Daniel from Minecraft Club again?" Kelli asks.

"Yeah." My hands are sweaty because I'm totally lying. *I hate this.* It's true that Daniel is at Minecraft Club right now—if you can call it a club when it's just a bunch of kids sitting in a room and playing on their devices with Ms. Moreno smoking their butts (no idea how she got so good at *Minecraft*). But it's not true that I need to pick him up. Daniel is going to walk the two doors down to dance rehearsal on his own as he always does. "My parents don't want him to have too much screen time, so I'm supposed to go make him do homework."

"I get it," Lauren says, making me feel even more guilty. "Being a big sister is important." She's an only child and, sometimes, she acts like a second big sister to Daniel.

"Right," Kelli says. "It's a pain to babysit when your little brother doesn't really need it and probably gets mad about it, but what can you do?" She's always stuck babysitting her little sister.

All this misplaced sympathy from my friends makes me squirm in discomfort. *Why am I lying to them?* Not for the first time, I wish I had just told them the truth in the first place—that I have to keep the film secret or else my parents might make me quit the school video competition to focus on the community center fundraiser, especially if they find out that I'm always late to dance rehearsals because of the film. Unlike my parents, Lauren and Kelli would probably understand, but I can't confess now. I've been lying to them too long. Plus, I don't want them to worry about the possibility of losing their screenwriter/director.

"Hey, I almost forgot," Kelli says, smoothing down the pleather material of her pants. "I'm almost done with your cosplay outfit, so make sure you ask your parents about Comic Con next weekend."

"I will," I promise. My parents have been so stressed about our Chinese school losing its home that I haven't wanted to bring up Comic Con, but I'm sure they'll let me go. After all, they owe me for Chinese dance. And I really, really want to go to Comic Con.

Kelli lifts her axe and holds it the way I had directed her to. Lauren gives Glenn a blinding smile before picking up her end of the spell book with Marissa. Everyone else takes their places too.

I hold up my tablet. "Ready. Three, two, one, and action."

I zoom in on Kelli and the others as they march purposefully down the hall to meet the villains, who saunter over with bared fangs.

This is going to be awesome.

Two takes later, I reluctantly call out, "Okay, five-minute break." I'd like to try for one more take, preferably one where the slayer's mentor didn't keep glancing over to the side while she's supposed to be helping cast a spell of protection for the slayer. At least the Fencing Team kept their word and stayed quiet during filming.

"Wow, that was so cool!" Glenn is saying to Lauren.

"Thanks!" She beams at them.

Normally, Kelli would be butting in on any discussion of a film she's starring in, but not this time. "Who wants to hit up the vending machine?" she calls out, leading the rest of the cast, except for Lauren, down the hall.

Smart. That will give Lauren and Glenn a little privacy—if it weren't for the rest of the Fencing Team. Most of them look like they're high schoolers or older, and the only one I recognize is Adam, a teenager who used to go to our Chinese school. *Good enough.*

"Hey, Adam," I call out, holding up my tablet. "While Lauren tells Glenn about our film, can I interview you and the rest of the team for . . . uh . . ." My mind races. A school project? Footage for a future movie? Research in case I somehow find myself in a fencing duel?

"Sure!" Adam says before I can come up with a believable reason.

I breathe a sigh of relief. It must be true that everyone secretly wants to be on camera. Even if the camera in question is a tablet being wielded by a twelve-year-old.

Then the rest of the team speaks up. "We can show you the practice room," one of them says.

"And we can explain the different types of foils!" another adds.

"Uh, okay." Panicked, I check the time again. I'm not going to get a third take on that scene unless I bag this fake Fencing Team interview and call everyone back from break *right* now.

But then Lauren shoots a meltingly grateful look at me before turning back to her conversation with Glenn. I can practically see the hearts in her eyes.

With a stifled sigh, I let the team usher me into their practice room. It smells like sweaty teenagers and the same lemon-scented stuff used to clean the Chinese school classrooms. "Let's do this," I say, holding up my tablet and hitting record. "So, what got you all into fencing?"

"Wuxia movies," Adam says without hesitation.

Wuxia? He's totally speaking my language. I love those magical Chinese martial arts movies too.

"Listen, Lily, I have an idea," he says excitedly. "I've watched every wuxia film out there and have been wanting to do sword fighting choreography forever. What do you think of the Fencing Team being extras in your film? We could do some choreographed sword fighting scenes!"

Everyone nods in eager agreement.

"That's really nice of you all." I hit pause on my tablet while I think of a way to let them down gently. "But I just don't think it's that kind of film. I mean, we don't have any sword fighting. Just staking vampires and cutting off demon heads with axes. You know, non-sword stuff."

"Oh." Adam's face falls. "Yeah, I guess that makes sense."

Feeling bad, I hit record again and angle my tablet toward the guy who wanted to talk about the different kinds of foils. "Now about those foils . . ." I prompt him.

As he launches into a lecture that looks like it's going to be long and detailed, I mentally kiss my chance at shooting another take of the scene for our film goodbye. Or getting to dance rehearsal on time.

Panting, I sprint down the hall of the community center. Have I ever been this late to dance rehearsal before? It was just that I *had* to try to get that hallway scene right.

Actually, that last take was pretty darn perfect. Tim's death scene and Kelli's axe moves were totally cool. The Fencing Team agreed. They even offered to help clean up. I do feel a bit bad about leaving everyone with all that fake blood, but I am *really* late. I round the corner like I'm nearing the finish line when—*Wham!*

My arms flail wildly as I try to keep my balance, but it's no use. I go down hard, landing painfully on my butt. My backpack soars through the air and papers fly everywhere.

"Oof!" Max says, staggering backward.

Again? What are the chances that I'd crash into him twice in one month? But this time, it isn't pennies that are strewn all over the floor. *My script!*

I leap to my feet and start frantically picking up the scattered pages.

"Here, let me help," Max offers.

"No need," I say desperately. "I've got it." The last thing I need is for him to see my script and put two and two together. . . .

"Hang on," he says, picking up a page and scanning it.

Darn. Too late. My stomach drops. "Give that back!"

"This is the screenplay for the film your friends were talking about at lunch the other day. Is this why you're always late to dance rehearsal? Wait. You're entering a video into Clarktown's Got Talent?"

Drat. "How did you know?"

"Come on! I've been competing with you for years. You think I haven't figured out how you work? Face it, Lily—I know you."

"You really are Maxistopheles Maxiavelli," I grumble even though it probably wasn't too hard to figure out what I was up to.

He just grins and flicks my screenplay with a finger. "It says 'Mephistopheles Machiavelli' here. I see you changed the name of your villain."

I snatch the page from his hand. "Well, I didn't want you to sue me for libel or anything."

"But seriously, why are you keeping your film a secret from your parents?"

"It's not like you've told your parents about dance rehearsals," I shoot back, trying to put the pages in order before giving up and cramming the whole mess into my backpack.

"Good point." He hands me a stray page. "Okay, I get why you're keeping your film a secret from your parents, but why didn't you want me to tell your friends about dance rehearsals the other day? And I'm guessing you haven't told Tina about the film either." He pauses. "What's that about?"

"It's complicated," I say glumly, but before I know it, I tell him *everything*. How bad I feel about Tina thinking I'm neglecting her and how maybe I haven't been as good a friend to her as I should. Then there's Lauren and Kelli. They get me like almost no one else does, but even they don't totally understand what Hong Chinese Academy or the community center means to me. Of course, the film means just as much to me, and I don't want to let my friends down or let them know that there's even a possibility of me quitting the Clarktown's Got Talent competition.

We're both going to be late to dance now, but he doesn't interrupt me until I wrap up. "So now I'm suddenly lying to everyone. And I *hate* it!" It seems that Max is the only person I'm not lying to. How did my arch-enemy become the person that I confide in?

"So, let me see if I understand," he says. "Your parents would want you to choose your Chinese school over your middle school, Tina would want you to choose the dance performance with her over the film with your other friends, and Lauren and Kelli would want you to choose the school competition over the community center fundraiser."

"That about sums it up."

"The question is," he says, "what do *you* want?"

"I want the magical ability to be in two places at once," I say promptly.

"That's not exactly what I meant. Let's pretend that superpowers and magical abilities are off the table. Then what do you want?"

I know what he's asking, but it's an impossible question. How do I choose between friends? How do I choose between the community center that's home to my family's Chinese school and the film that my friends are counting on me to make? It's like asking which vital organ I'd rather do without. "Well, if magic isn't an option, I'll settle for just one less thing to worry about."

"I have an idea about that." He clears his throat. "How about a truce?"

"A truce?" I'm so surprised that I actually think I must have misheard him.

"Yeah. I mean, we've been fighting since fifth grade."

"You started it by reading four Goosebump's books for the One Thousand Books Reading Challenge!"

"I was just doing my part," he says with a smirk.

My chin lifts. "I had it covered."

"Uh huh. If I hadn't shown up, you would have decided to read *War and Peace* after you finished whatever gigantic book you were reading, and then you could have kissed that victory pizza party goodbye."

"I told you—that was the last book in a series I started during the summer!" My teeth ache from gritting them so hard. "Besides, I read as many books as you did without reading Goosebumps or the CatStronauts."

"Do not hate on the CatStronauts. Who doesn't love graphic novels about cats in space?"

He's got me there. I *do* love those sassy and adorable space-faring cats—I'm not dead inside. "I'm just saying that *I* didn't read only books with pictures and large font sizes."

"You did know that the point was to win, right?"

"Are you questioning my competitive spirit?" I ask dangerously.

"Never," he says. "Look, don't get me wrong—competing with you has been fun." He flashes me a grin. "But think of what we could do if we joined forces."

I can't help but consider it. It's true that once Max lit a fire under me in fifth grade, I read faster than I ever had; together, Max and I got our class to a thousand books before our nearest competitors had even reached five hundred.

Maybe it is time to call a truce. Besides, Max is right that I can't afford unnecessary distractions right now. I stand up straight and look him in the eye. "Okay. But I have some conditions." I hold up a finger. "One, you promise not to tell Lauren and Kelli about me performing Chinese dance for the fundraiser." I raise another finger. "Two, we still pretend to be mortal enemies when Lauren and Kelli are around." I don't need Kelli jumping to more false conclusions about my so-called crush on him. A third finger goes up. "Three, you can't tell Tina about me working on the film with Lauren and Kelli."

"Is that all?" Max asks with a glint in his eye. "Are you sure there isn't a secret you're forgetting about? Maybe you want me to keep quiet about a homework scam you're running at school or something."

"Ha, ha." I glare at him. "Maybe I should add a 'no snarky comment' clause to our truce."

He grins. "Our truce wouldn't last the day!"

"A day?" I scoff. "It wouldn't last a minute!" A reluctant smile tugs at my mouth. "Do we have a truce or not?"

"Lily Hong, I agree to your conditions." He sticks out his hand. "Truce."

"Max Zhang, I hereby call a halt to hostilities as long as the previously-named terms are honored," I say solemnly.

He chokes on laughter and sputters, "Seriously? This is an agreement between seventh graders—not warring countries."

Since we didn't include the non-snark clause in our truce, I let it slide.

"Truce," I say.

Everyone stops and stares when Max and I come into the auditorium together . . . fifteen minutes late.

"You were doing so much better about getting to rehearsal earlier, Lily." Vivienne is actually wringing her hands. "And you, Max! You've never been late before! What happened?" She raises her eyes to the ceiling as if praying to the heavens for answers.

I feel bad about getting Max in trouble too, but he just smiles at Vivienne like the star suck-up—I mean, *student*, that he is. At least I didn't call him a suck-up out loud. Old habits are hard to break.

Tina sidles up to me. "What's going on with you two?"

I gave her one of Ms. Zhang's pineapple cakes last week as proof that I really did spy on Max and wasn't lying to her (about that, anyway). She felt bad about accusing me of lying to her (except that I am), and now we're good. Sort of. As long as I don't think too hard about my lies. "I'll tell you later," I whisper, "but the short version— Max is no longer the worst."

"It's my fault," Max is saying to Vivienne. "I was telling Lily about an idea Daniel and I came up with."

Wait. What idea?

Daniel walks over. "Oh, you told her about it?" He gives me a nervous look.

Um, Daniel knows about this too?

"An idea for the lion dance?" Vivienne's eyebrows rise.

"Sort of." Max turns to Daniel. "Go ahead. Tell her."

Daniel takes a deep breath. "I don't want to be a lion dancer anymore."

Is this my fault? My gut cramps with guilt. Did I tease my brother about being the butt of the lion one too many times? It's just that I'm jealous of all the acrobatic moves he gets to do. Although . . . to tell the truth, Daniel's not that great at those moves. Maybe I shouldn't mention that. "You shouldn't quit, Daniel," I say. "I mean, Max wasn't even hurt when you accidentally tripped him that last time." Eek. That sounded better in my head. More encouraging and less . . . judgy.

Ignoring me, Daniel runs over to the pile of extra fans on a table. Grabbing two fans, he snaps them open almost as gracefully as Vivienne herself—and starts doing these amazing flips and flourishes with them like he's been doing fan dancing all his life.

All the kids start cheering, but I'm too surprised to join in. What's happening? How did Daniel suddenly become a fan-dancing superstar?

Then I notice the proud expression on Max's face. *Ah*. I guess I'm not the only one he's been helping with the fans. A warm, fuzzy feeling fills my heart as I watch my little brother utterly *nail* the fan dance. Max isn't the only one who's bursting with pride in Daniel.

He wraps up the dance with a rapid flutter and flourish combo that I *still* haven't mastered, and everyone goes wild with clapping and whooping.

Even Vivienne looks impressed, but her face clouds over. "But who will dance the tail of the lion?"

"I can do the tail," Max offers. He catches my eye. "And Lily can be the head."

My jaw drops. *Whaaat?* Then I remember the excuse Max gave for us being late. I snap my mouth shut. Right. He's supposed to have already explained this idea to me. "Uh, sure! I can dance the head of the lion. That's what I said when Max told me about it earlier. Which is why we were late. Obviously."

Max shoots me a look that I have no problem

deciphering as *How are you so bad at this?* He's not wrong. In fact, it's a miracle I haven't been caught yet in one of my many, many lies.

Vivienne's expression shifts from despairing to thoughtful. "It could work." Under her breath, but just loud enough to hear, she murmurs, "It certainly can't make things worse." I'm not totally sure whether she means Daniel or me. We're both pretty awful in our current roles.

"Daniel," she says, "you can join the fan dancers. Tina, you're replacing Lily as the lead fan dancer." Julia sighs but doesn't argue. She knows Tina is the better dancer.

Finally, Vivienne turns to Max and me. "Max will dance the tail, and Lily will dance the head when you do the lifts. For the other parts of the routine, you'll switch."

For the first time, it hits me that I'm going to be a *freaking* lion dancer. Excitement fizzes up in me. How cool! And I owe it to . . . Max?

He's definitely not the worst anymore.

FIFTEEN

DANIEL AND I ARE HAVING a race to set the dining room table, which we only use when we have guests. I've got plates and chopsticks, and he has cups and napkins. I slam down a plate at each place setting and then toss the chopsticks next to each plate. "Done!" I announce, throwing up my hands like they do when time is called on those cooking competition shows.

Daniel has placed all the cups, but he still has three napkins left to go. "That's not fair! I'd be done if I didn't have to fold the napkins in half."

"Fine. I'll take cups and napkins next time, and I'll still beat you. You might be a better fan dancer, but I still rule at table setting."

Daniel sticks his tongue out at me, but then he says, "That was pretty cool of Max today, wasn't it? To talk Vivienne into letting us trade parts?"

"It was." I'm surprised by how easily I agree. Maybe my war with Max really is over.

Mom comes into the dining room and shakes her head. "Why are the chopsticks so messy? They're not even on the napkins!" She's not usually this picky about how I set the table, but then again, tonight's not a usual dinner.

"I'll fix it!" I say quickly, straightening a pair of chopsticks.

Vivienne is coming over for dinner, and Mom's stress is off the scale. She and Dad have been cooking all day. In fact, Dad is in the kitchen right now, chopping up vegetables for a last-minute addition because Mom decided that *eleven* dishes weren't enough.

Even Daniel seems to notice the tension in the air. Instead of demanding a rematch because my chopsticks were placed crookedly, he quietly finishes up with the napkins.

It's actually a little weird Mom's so worked up over this. I mean, she and Vivienne went out for dinner just last week. And from what I could tell (from eavesdropping on her debriefing with Dad), that went okay. Mom even said that they had "reached an understanding." So why is she so tense about having Vivienne over for dinner tonight? Mom did drop the fact that Vivienne is pretty wealthy, so maybe she just wants to impress her rich frenemy. But twelve dishes for six people is still next-level social anxiety.

Wait a minute. I stop cold in the middle of picking up a pair of chopsticks. When Mom told us to set the table for six, I was so focused on beating Daniel that I didn't do the math. Mom, Dad, Daniel, me, and Vivienne are only *five* people. "Um, who else besides Viv—I mean, Ms. Hou is coming to dinner?"

Mom's mouth puckers. "Your auntie Li."

I flash back to Vivienne darting out of the practice room and how I caught a glimpse of Auntie Li afterward. And how upset Vivienne seemed when she returned. *Oh.* No wonder Mom is stress-cooking. "Does Auntie Li know Ms. Hou is going to be here?"

"Of course she knows." Her face is unreadable.

"It's just that there seems to be some, you know— *serious* history between the two of them." Is my mom trying to get them to call a truce by inviting them both over for dinner?

"Daniel," she says, ignoring me. "Can you bring out the nice serving spoons for the hot dishes?"

"We won't have enough for all the food!" he protests.

"Just get what we have!"

Mom turns back to me after Daniel leaves. "I invited Vivienne over to thank her for her generous offer to treat your dance class to a performance of the Fenghuang Performers in Seattle," she says firmly. "And I invited Auntie Li over to thank her for going along on the field trip to chaperone. That's all."

Hold up a minute . . . field trip? "Vivienne didn't say anything about a field trip during rehearsal today."

"I asked her not to say anything until I sent out the permission slips to the parents. You'll be staying for a whole weekend in a hotel in downtown Seattle, and I wanted to give the parents a heads-up before we told the children."

Dread snakes into my stomach. "When is it?"

"Next weekend."

The bottom falls out from under me. I knew it. This is just my rotten luck. "That's the same weekend as Comic Con! I was going to ask you and Dad tonight if I could go with Lauren and Kelli!"

"I'm sorry," she says sympathetically, "but we can't turn down Vivienne's kind gift. Your friends will understand."

I wouldn't bet on it. Plus, I really wanted to go to the Emerald City Comic Con. This would have been the first time for all of us. I throw the chopsticks I'm holding onto the dining table with more force than necessary, and they land even more crookedly than before.

Mom has gone into the kitchen to help Daniel scrounge up enough serving spoons for twelve dishes, so she doesn't see the mess I'm making out of the place settings.

With a sigh, I fix the chopsticks.

This. Is. Epically. Unfair.

Auntie Li marches into our house, briefly greets Dad, and sails right past Vivienne into the kitchen—*without taking her shoes off.*

Yikes. I almost drop the pot I'm supposed to be rinsing out at the sink. Daniel freezes in place with soapsuds dripping from his hands, and Mom stops chopping green onions at the counter.

"Lily. Daniel. Sara." Auntie Li says our names grimly, like she's come to be debriefed about an asteroid crashing into Earth or something equally catastrophic.

Carefully, I set down the pot. "Hi, Auntie Li." I try to avoid staring at her shoes.

"Do you need to warm that up?" Mom asks, nodding toward the saran-wrapped tray Auntie Li is carrying.

"No." She all but slams the tray on the counter.

Daniel and I exchange startled looks when we see what she's brought. Thin, deflated, and obviously store-bought jiaozi. *Double yikes.* Mom always makes her homemade jiaozi for special dinners, and Auntie Li knows it. Bringing grocery store jiaozi to one of Mom's dinners is like giving a toy lightsaber to an actual Jedi.

Mom narrows her eyes at Auntie Li. "If you don't need to warm those . . ." She trails off like she can't quite bring herself to call those pathetic dumplings *jiaozi.* ". . . then you might as well hang out in the living room with the others."

In the living room, Dad and Vivienne are talking in hushed voices, but they keep glancing into the kitchen, so it's not hard to imagine what they're discussing.

"No thanks." Auntie Li scowls and grabs a handful of dirty utensils. "I'll help Lily and Daniel wash up."

Seriously, what went down between Vivienne and Auntie Li? And if Mom thinks she can fix this with dinner and a field trip, then she's delusional.

"Give your auntie Li some of the fish, Lily," Mom says, gesturing to the gigantic platter of fish in front of me. Little pieces of green onions and ginger are floating in the sauce, and it smells as good as it looks.

I reach for the serving spoon, but Auntie Li shakes her head. "I can get the fish myself." To prove it, she grabs the spoon and serves me a piece of fish and some sauce. Then, instead of serving Vivienne, sitting next to her, she helps herself.

I frown. Some rules (like taking off your shoes inside) are obvious, but then there's keqi rules—the changing expectations of what's considered polite in some situations but not others (like how it's sometimes polite for my parents to insist on paying for everyone at a restaurant, but it might be insulting to do that with close friends and family). It's super confusing. And that's why I'm not sure if Auntie Li just gave Vivienne a major snub or not. I glance at Mom, but she's calmly passing a bamboo steamer over to Daniel, so maybe it's okay.

Then Dad, sitting on the other side of Vivienne, clears his throat in that way he does when he gets nervous. "Here, Vivienne, try some of Sara's jiaozi." He quickly snags a few from the platter in front of him and puts them on her plate.

Wait a minute . . . I peer suspiciously at the sad, droopy dumplings on her plate, and my heart goes cold. No way are those Mom's jiaozi.

Daniel seems to be completely oblivious to the drama unfolding right next to him as he uncovers the bamboo steamer and takes a few fat, pillowy jiaozi, just oozing with juicy meat and spices. *Those* are Mom's jiaozi. Dad must have come to the same realization because his eyes lock onto the clearly superior jiaozi, and he immediately turns bright red. I don't blame him. I'd feel the same way if I had accidentally "credited" Mom with grocery store dumplings.

Vivienne uses her chopsticks to poke delicately at one of the jiaozi on her plate, the top edges already dry and curling and the sides caving in on themselves because there's not even enough filling to hold the dumpling upright. "You made these, Sara?" she asks doubtfully before adding, "They look delicious." At least Vivienne is still trying to be keqi.

Mom eyes the shriveled jiaozi on Vivienne's plate like they're alien spawn, and I suck in my breath. Is she going to take the fall for the subpar jiaozi or rat out her best friend?

"I brought them," Auntie Li announces. "They were on sale at the store. Two bags for the price of one."

I wince. Mom's reputation is saved, but now Vivienne will know exactly how much Auntie Li resents being here.

Vivienne's face sets. "Well, I know Sara made that fish. It looks wonderful." She picks up her plate and hands it to Auntie Li. "Ellen, can I trouble you for some?"

"Of course." Frost practically drips from Auntie Li's voice. She puts some fish on Vivienne's plate without adding sauce. The fish looks all sad and pale next to the even sadder and paler jiaozi.

Vivienne keeps the plate outstretched. "Sauce too, please."

Her lips pressed tightly together, Auntie Li dumps so much on her plate that the flimsy dumplings bob up and down like little white boats on a sea of sauce. "Is that enough?"

"Yes, thank you." Vivienne's eyes flash. "The jiaozi you brought look like they could use some flavoring anyway." *Gulp. Definitely not keqi.*

The dinner has barely even started, and both Auntie Li and Vivienne have declared war. Poor Mom. I'm still mad at her for keeping me from Comic Con, but I'd be a terrible person if I took any joy from this epic disaster of a dinner.

Daniel finally seems to notice the tension in the room and sends me a pleading look like he's asking me what to do. *Heck if I know.* When an adult like Auntie Li is deliberately breaking all the rules, all we kids can do is duck and cover. I give Daniel a resigned shrug.

Mom is staring sadly at the table loaded with her twelve mouthwatering dishes like she can't believe that all her peacemaking efforts are going to waste, but then her jaw firms, and she says to Daniel, "Go get your *auntie* Hou a new plate." He leaps up from the dining room table and scurries to the kitchen.

A muscle twitches in Auntie Li's cheek when Mom refers to Vivienne as "Auntie Hou." She takes a deep breath, sends Mom a resentful glare . . . and lays down her weapon of choice (a.k.a. the serving spoon). *Score one for Mom.* But then Auntie Li turns to *me*. "So, Lily, how is school?"

I blink in surprise. Usually, her questions about school are pretty specific—like what did I think of the surprise twist in a book or what did Lauren's water sample analysis reveal? She doesn't normally ask weird, generic questions. "Uh, fine, I guess."

"Any big projects or tests coming up?"

"Yeah, I guess so." I'm used to this kind of inquisition from relatives who visit from China once every two or three years, but Auntie Li has known me all my life. This is clearly a ploy to avoid talking to Vivienne.

Mom sighs. She's obviously not thrilled about Auntie Li completely ignoring Vivienne, but I can't spare Mom any sympathy. *I'm* the one who has to endure the standard adult school interrogation.

And Auntie Li isn't even paying attention to my responses. When I tell her that my science teacher is making our class dissect frogs next week and I'm afraid I'll be the kid who throws up (there's one every year), she just says, "That's nice."

"Vivienne," Mom says, cutting across my description of Joey Howser's projectile vomit last year, "do you remember when we used to go to Clarktown Diner for breakfast every weekend? You'll never believe it, but it's still there. Ellen and I still go there sometimes."

"And what did you get on your report card?" Auntie Li asks me.

Really? She already knows I got straight As. Just to test if anyone's paying attention, I say, "Mostly As, but I got a B in one class." At any other time, my fake-news B would've gotten everyone's attention, but it doesn't even make a ripple now.

Mom doesn't bother to glance in my direction as she fills the clean plate Daniel brings her, pointedly avoiding the grocery store dumplings. "We should all go there for breakfast sometime."

"Good job," Auntie Li says to me.

"The omelets at Clarktown Diner are really *eggcellent*."

Dad's cringey joke earns a grateful look from Mom. He's probably trying to make up for what I'm going to refer to as "the great jiaozi mistake" from now on.

Daniel takes the refilled plate from Mom and passes it to Dad. "Wow. That's pretty corny even for you, Dad."

Vivienne laughs a little too hard as she accepts the new plate from Dad. "*I* think it's funny."

"James isn't the only one who's funny," Mom says. "Remember, Ellen, when Vivienne did stand-up comedy at Clarktown Pub's amateur night?"

"No, I don't remember." Then Auntie Li asks me, "How did other students do on their report cards?"

"Everyone did fine, and I know that because I personally examined each kid's report card." My sarcasm doesn't even get a raised eyebrow from the adults although Daniel does roll his eyes at me. I sigh. "Yup, honor roll all around." No response at all. Nothing. Zip. Zero. Which is also what Mom is getting from her attempts to draw Auntie Li into a discussion about old times.

Maybe *now* Mom will give up on her hopeless plan to make peace between Vivienne and Auntie Li. Guilty longing rises in my chest. And maybe Mom will cancel the Chinese school field trip this weekend, so I can go to Comic Con after all.

"I remember that comedy act!" Vivienne says suddenly. "God, I was terrible." This time, her laugh sounds like her real one, all spontaneous and bubbly.

Auntie Li's eyes dart over to her, and an odd expression crosses her face. She's looking at Vivienne like she doesn't think she's terrible at all—just the opposite. In the next moment, Auntie Li has turned back to me and is asking another question about school, her face carefully blank. But I know what I saw.

My jaw drops as understanding explodes in my brain like a hundred fireworks. So *that's* why my mom invited them both over for dinner tonight and is making Auntie Li chaperone us on the field trip!

My mother is trying to set up Vivienne and Auntie Li. Or maybe she's trying to get them back together again.

Luckily, Auntie Li doesn't seem to notice my stunned reaction. She's too busy pretending to ignore the conversation between Vivienne and my parents.

"Is Clarktown Pub still around?" Vivienne asks.

"No, it's an ice cream parlor now," Dad says. "Before that, I think it was a microbrewery and then a fusion restaurant. Nothing seemed to stick before the ice cream parlor."

Vivienne nods. "Like that skating rink. What is that now?"

"The clubhouse at the Palisades," Mom says dryly. "I'm sure they tore down the original structure before building there, but none of us have been inside the Palisades, so who knows?"

Except that I *do* know. I squirm uncomfortably as I

think of my secret spy mission into the Palisades. Mom's right. The old skating rink had been an old, boarded-up building, and there's nothing left of it in the sleek and modern clubhouse.

Vivienne lifts an eyebrow. "Really? How do you feel about that, Sara?" Mom's feelings about the Zhangs are so obvious that even dreamy, scattered Vivienne has noticed.

"Arthur Murphy runs the ice cream shop, actually," Mom says, evading her question. "Lily is friends with his daughter."

"She's also friends with Sam's daughter," Dad adds.

"How lovely!" Vivienne says. "Wait a minute—didn't Sam tell knock-knock jokes at that amateur comedy night?" She shakes her head with a smile.

Yup. That sounds like Lauren's dad, all right. I'm surprised *my* dad didn't get up and join him.

Auntie Li breaks my train of thought by suddenly whipping around to face Vivienne. "What was that joke *you* told?" Her voice is cold. "Oh yes, I remember now. 'Clarktown is so boring that you couldn't wait to leave it.' "

Um, that doesn't sound like a joke. My skin goes all hot and itchy, like I'm about to break out into nervous hives. Everyone else seems to feel the tension too, and even Daniel stops fidgeting.

The smile slides right off Vivienne's face. "If I recall

correctly that joke was: 'Clarktown is so small that it's not even on the map.'" Her eyes are hard. "Not a great joke, but to be fair, it was a tough audience. Maybe that's what drove me out of Clarktown. A tough audience."

Ouch. The room goes so quiet that Daniel's sharp cough sounds way too loud. Auntie Li has gone pale.

I'm not sure why Vivienne left, but I have a feeling that it wasn't because of a failed comedy routine.

"That would have been a silly reason to leave." Mom's voice sounds strained.

"Yes, it would have been," Vivienne says quietly, glancing at Auntie Li. "Actually, it's hard to remember why I left. In all the time I was away, I only remembered the reasons for coming back."

I start to breathe again. Maybe Mom's matchmaking plan isn't so hopeless after all. I had thought that Auntie Li and Vivienne were like Max and me—mortal enemies from the beginning, but it turns out they were something else completely.

The color creeps back into Auntie Li's face, and I'm waiting for her to throw herself into her former enemy's arms and proclaim her undying love . . . okay, maybe the last isn't likely, and they're not really enemies, but can I help it if enemies-to-lovers happens to be my absolute *favorite* romantic plotline? Give me a book with two characters fighting their feelings for each other while dueling to the death or competing in a bake-off, and I will one hundred percent read it. So it's no surprise that my heart is going all squishy to think of Auntie Li and Vivienne secretly longing for each other while pretending to hate each other.

Oh, darn. Now I'm suddenly rooting for Mom's plan to work.

Then Auntie Li asks me for the third time tonight, "How is school going, Lily?"

Vivienne's face falls.

Argh! How can Auntie Li not see that Vivienne is still desperately in love with her? "School's fine." It's the same answer I gave Auntie Li the last two times.

"Still fighting with that Zhang boy?"

I practically choke on a bite of rice. "What?"

For the first time tonight, it feels like I have Auntie Li's attention. She smiles. "I take it that things are better with you two?"

My face grows hot. Just because Max and I aren't enemies anymore doesn't mean that we're . . . anything else.

I take a deep breath and force myself to sound chill. "Yeah, it's better now."

SIXTEEN

—

THAT NIGHT, DAD COMES INTO my bedroom as he always does, but instead of just saying goodnight and leaving, he sits down on the end of my bed. "Your mother told me that you have to miss Comic Con with your friends next weekend," he says awkwardly.

I sit up in bed. "I don't want to talk about it unless you and Mom have decided to let me skip the Chinese school field trip and go to Comic Con instead."

He shakes his head. "Sorry, Lily."

It's not his fault, but I slide back under the covers and say grumpily, "Goodnight, then."

He looks at me in silence for a moment. "You know, it's been a while since I've told you the phoenix story."

Uh huh. A story about sacrifice for the greater good. *Subtle, Dad, real subtle.*

But that's not totally fair to Dad. After all, he's been

telling me that story about his childhood home in China since I was a little kid, and it has been a while since he's told it. Plus, I've never turned down a chance to hear "The Phoenix and Her City," and I'm not about to start now. "Fine," I say, "but make it quick and tell it the right way. Don't have the monkey king suddenly show up with Scooby-Doo, offering the townspeople magical peanut butter and jelly sandwiches or whatever." My dad has been known to do some weird mash-ups in his telling of the story—and this is coming from *me*, who doesn't think twice about pairing a Medusa myth with Lizzo in the opening scene of a film.

He smiles and starts the way he always does. "The story of 'The Phoenix and Her City' is about Yinchuan, a beautiful city on the edge of a desert. I was born there, you know?"

"Wo zhidao," I reply as I always do. *I know.*

"Many Hui still live in Yinchuan today. That's our people, you know."

"Wo zhidao."

From there, the story can go in any direction. One time, Dad even brought in Alexander Hamilton and tried to *rap*. I'm still scarred from that.

"Okay, but did you know that the phoenix was friends with Iron Man?"

"Dad! You promised!"

"Fine!" He throws up his hands. "Yinchuan was a

beautiful city, but every year, the desert took over a little bit more, and before long, the city was in danger of being swallowed by sand."

I burrow into my blankets and wiggle my toes happily. *Yes.* This is what I wanted.

"Luckily, there was a goose who offered to take a message from the people of the city to the phoenix, pleading with the bird of happiness to save their city." This isn't Dad adding random weird stuff again—it's actually a part of the story. "The goose flew all the way to the Helan Mountains, where seven phoenix sisters lived."

"And the youngest phoenix was so moved that she agreed to help the people of Yinchuan even though her sisters begged her not to go," I say eagerly.

"Hey! Who's telling the story?" Dad says, but he's grinning because he likes it when I jump in to tell parts.

"Anyway," he says, "the phoenix came to Yinchuan, bringing the rains, and the city prospered. Unfortunately, Yinchuan's new fortune drew unwanted attention from jealous and corrupt officials who wanted to plunder the city for its riches." His voice drops dramatically. "The phoenix knew the only way to protect the city she loved would require a great sacrifice, so she turned her own body into fortifications for the city. Her eyes became towers, her claws became the wall, and her heart became the drum tower. Then one day, a mighty villain came—"

"If you say Thanos or Darkseid or any other

supervillain, I swear I'm going to scream."

"A thief," Dad says grudgingly. "An ordinary, nameless thief with no superpowers comes to the city to steal its riches, but he knows the phoenix guards the city, so . . ."

"He kills her." Even though it's only a story and one that I've heard hundreds of times, an ache creeps into my throat.

"That's not the end," Dad says, patting me on the leg. Usually, there's a bunch more quests and pop culture references before he wraps up, but tonight, he gets right to the line he always ends with, no matter how many random fictional characters he throws into the mix. "The phoenix will rise again to bring happiness to the city she loves."

Trying to hide my sniffles, I wipe my eyes on the edge of my blanket.

"Goodnight, Lily," Dad says, and starts to stand up.

That's when I remember something I wanted to ask him. "Viv . . . I mean, Ms. Hou said that she'd heard of 'The Phoenix and Her City.' How does she know the story?"

"Imagine Vivienne remembering that." He laughs. "She was there when I first told your mother that story. So was your auntie Li."

"What?" My eyes widen. "You have to tell me more." Here's my chance to find out what went down between Mom, Auntie Li, and Vivienne.

"There's not much to tell." He sits back down. "You know I came to Clarktown to teach Chinese at the community college, right?"

I nod. Dad's been teaching that one Chinese class every quarter for as long as I can remember.

"Well," he says, "when I first came to Clarktown, I was planning to just stay for the school year. But then I met your mother, and I couldn't imagine being anywhere without her. I thought I could convince her to move with me to Seattle or some other city where I could get a better teaching job, but she wouldn't leave Clarktown."

Huh. I never knew that Dad had tried to talk Mom into leaving Clarktown. The thing is—I've never even heard Dad *hint* about moving away from Clarktown. Not when the community center basement got flooded, not when my big-shot uncle offered Dad a job in California—not even now, when we might lose our school for good. "So what happened?"

His eyes become unfocused like he's lost in a memory. "I was out with your mother, your auntie Li, and Vivienne one night. That's when I told them the story of the phoenix. I think I was trying to make some point about the youngest phoenix being brave enough to leave the nest or something like that, but your mother wouldn't change her mind."

Yeah, that part isn't surprising. Mom never misses a town event, knows half the people by name, and goes to book club with the same friends she's had since she was twelve. Dad would've had better luck moving a skyscraper than prying Mom from Clarktown. "What did she say?" I ask.

"She said that even though she wasn't born in Clarktown, she loved the city and its people as much as the phoenix loved Yinchuan." He smiles. "That was it for me. Clarktown was your mother's home, and she was *my* home, so I had to stay."

My heart flutters. That's so darned romantic even if it *is* my own parents. I sigh with delight. "So, that's when Vivienne heard the story? It must have made an impression if she still remembers it."

Dad's smile slips. "I wonder if it made the right impression."

I sit up in bed, sensing something juicy. "What do you mean?"

He hesitates and then says, "It's probably nothing, but Vivienne left Clarktown the next day."

"Really? So she picked up on that whole heavy-handed 'bird leaving the nest' metaphor you were hitting Mom over the head with?"

He gets a pained look on his face, and I say hastily, "I'm sure that's not why Vivienne left Clarktown. Anyway, she's back now, isn't she?"

"Yes, she is." His expression is still troubled. "I just hope she'll stay."

I peer at my dad. "Were you ever sorry?" I mean, he still teaches just that one class at the community college plus Saturday class at our school, and he's stuck in Clarktown—a city with a yearly school video competition and a run-down community center as the main attractions.

"Never." He reaches over and ruffles my hair, which I normally hate, but I let it slide—since we're having a moment and all. "This place has a way of growing on you," he says, and I can tell he means it.

I think about the whole town turning out to help us clean up after the community center basement flooded, and I get why Mom wouldn't leave Clarktown and why Dad doesn't regret staying. My heart turns hopeful. Vivienne must have wanted to come back. I mean, she's not here just to teach dance to a bunch of kids who can barely hold a fan (okay, that's just me). "I think Vivienne knows how special Clarktown is."

"I hope so," Dad says.

Then my brain starts buzzing with an idea. Maybe there's a way to help everyone get what they want—Auntie Li, Vivienne . . . and me.

SEVENTEEN

Okay. I can do this. It's Saturday morning, and my luck finally seems to be changing. The downtown hotel we checked into last night is practically next door to the convention center where Comic Con is being held.

My tablet on the hotel nightstand dings (I must be the only seventh grader who doesn't have a phone), and I lunge for it.

Tina, who had been sound asleep in the next bed, lifts her head from her pillow and says groggily, "Who's texting you this early?"

"Just a friend," I say distractedly as I read the text from Kelli.

> The eagle has landed.

Kelli is taking this secret spy stuff a little too seriously.

I mean, I'm sneaking out to Comic Con, not plotting a heist. My heart twists. Would she be so eager to help if she knew everything I conveniently left out when I told my friends about this field trip?

Lauren's text follows almost immediately.

> We're in the lobby.

"Uh, Tina, I need to run down to the lobby to get . . ." My imagination fails me when I stop to consider what I would need to get at eight in the morning. ". . . a newspaper."

"Don't they deliver those to the room?"

"Do they?" I curse my lack of experience with hotels. "Well, I'm just going to check then." I slip on my sneakers and grab my backpack.

Tina rises on her elbows. "Why are you up already and dressed? We're not supposed to meet the others for another hour, and you *hate* getting up early."

Darn. Tina knows me too well. I'm the last one up at every overnight Chinese "camp" at the community center. "I'm trying something new!" I call out over my shoulder as I dash out the door.

Right at the doorway is a newspaper. I scoop it up, tuck it under my arm as my alibi, and take the elevator down to the lobby—where I do an immediate double take.

Kelli and Lauren are wearing sunglasses and baseball caps in addition to their Comic Con outfits. The combination is . . . striking. Kelli has on a brightly striped sweater and overalls as Willow, Buffy's best friend (from the pre-witch episodes), and Lauren has on wide-legged red silk pants and a big silver choker as Kendra, the slayer. According to the frantic play-by-play texts Lauren and I got late last night, Kelli just finished making our costumes on time, but that doesn't explain the sunglasses and caps.

Before I can ask, Lauren says, "The 'disguises' were Kelli's idea, and it was just easier to go along with it."

"Lily can't be seen with us," Kelli says in a low voice. "In fact, we should act like we're not talking to her." She sidles up next to me, facing the other direction. "Like this."

"Right," I say. "Sunglasses indoors and avoiding eye contact. That's a *lot* less conspicuous."

Still looking away from me and pitching her voice low, Kelli says, "I have the package. Put your backpack down, walk fifty paces ahead, and then—"

"Seriously? We don't have time for this!" Lauren grabs a plastic bag from Kelli and hands it to me. "That's your costume. Find a way to sneak away from your field trip, change into it, and then meet us at Comic Con later. Here's your ticket." She gives me a white envelope. "My mom is waiting outside to take us to Comic Con, so we have to go now." She gives me a hug, ignoring Kelli's gasp at how she's blatantly breaking spy protocol. "Good luck, Lily. Hope to see you soon."

She drags away Kelli, who's muttering about Lauren being a spoilsport.

Phase One is complete. Now for the hard part. Phase Two.

Phase Two is not going well.

It's already lunchtime, and I still haven't figured out a way to sneak away. My tablet dings, and Tina nudges me. "I think you're getting another text."

"Right." I pull my tablet out of my backpack and try to be subtle about angling it away from her.

It's from Lauren.

> No cell phone service in the convention center. Came outside to text. r u on your way? Eliza Dushku AND James Marsters just made a surprise appearance. They're leaving in 20 minutes. HURRY!

Noooo! I gasp out loud. The actress who played Faith, the slayer who fights her way to redemption, and the actor who played Spike, the vampire with a secret heart of gold, are *both* at Comic Con?!

"What's wrong?" Tina asks.

"Nothing." My jaw sets. I have to get to the convention center.

It wouldn't be too hard if it were just Vivienne. I could slip past her not-so-eagle eyes without a problem, but Auntie Li is our other chaperone, and she's drawn up a touristy itinerary designed to fill every spare minute until the Fenghuang dance performance tonight. We've already done the Seattle Wheel, the Monorail, and the Space Needle—and that was all before noon.

Right now, we're back at the hotel for their lunch buffet and Auntie Li is chatting up the concierge in case there's an obscure tourist attraction she might have missed.

Avoiding Tina's curious gaze, I drop my tablet in my backpack and say to Auntie Li, "Clarktown is only an hour away from Seattle, so it's not like we're actually tourists. Why do we need to do all this stuff?" I'm fully aware that I sound like a whiny five-year-old. It's definitely not one of my finer moments, but I'm desperate.

Clearly unmoved, she replies, "This field trip is supposed to be about experiencing culture. So that's what we're going to do."

Yeah, right. She just wants to fill up our schedule so she's too busy to interact with Vivienne. So far, she's succeeded in limiting her conversation with Vivienne to a grand total of two sentences. "Yes, my room is nice" and "The Space Needle is next on our itinerary." Both were in response to direct questions from Vivienne.

Maybe it's a lost cause, but there's no way I'm going to be stuck with the guys tossing fish in Pike Place Market while my friends are showing off their cosplay outfits to Eliza Dushku and James Marsters of *Buffy* fame.

Time for Plan B—I'm going to have to work on Vivienne.

Vivienne, elegant in a black jumpsuit splashed with vivid orange and hot pink, says, "Come along, children! It's time for lunch." She sweeps past Auntie Li, who's gone back to pumping the concierge for information. The air between them is practically sizzling with tension.

Vivienne leads us from the lobby into the hotel restaurant and waves us toward the lunch bar. "It's all you can eat! Have fun!"

Normally, I'd be all over a buffet, but I've got a plan to put into motion. Mom's not the only matchmaker in the family.

Okay, I have ulterior motives, but really, it's a win-win. Auntie Li and Vivienne get to figure out whatever is between them—and be too distracted to notice my absence. And I get to go to Comic Con with my friends.

It's *obvious* that Vivienne is dying for some alone time with Auntie Li, and despite my aunt's schedule packed with fish tossing and underground tours—I suspect the feeling is mutual. I haven't forgotten the look on Auntie Li's face at dinner the other night.

Tina tugs on my arm. "Hurry up! If Julia gets there first, there won't be any of the good stuff left!"

"Go on ahead," I tell her. "I have to ask Vivienne something."

She looks torn, but at that moment, Julia squeals, "Ooh, tempura shrimp!"

"Don't take too long," Tina calls out over her shoulder as she races to the buffet table.

Once I'm left with Vivienne, I don't know what to say. It's not like I can come right out and ask, *So, what are your intentions toward my auntie Li?*

Max could probably figure out some clever way to throw the two of them together, but he's not here. Of course, he wanted to come, but there's the little problem of him not actually attending Hong Chinese Academy. Vivienne might be willing to keep Max's part in our performance on the down-low, but there's no way Auntie Li would keep that secret from my mother. So—no Max this weekend.

"Don't you want to get some food?" Vivienne asks me.

"What's going on between you and Auntie Li?" I blurt out. *Smooth. Real smooth, Lily.*

Vivienne just stares at me blankly without speaking . . . which is a really unnerving reaction from a woman who practically fell into a swoon when Max showed her a picture of his pet rat (from his film *Of Mice and Mazes*). I think he had some idea of incorporating Theseus (that's the name of his rat) into the lion dance, but Vivienne's reaction nixed that idea.

Now she says stonily, "Nothing." Then sadness cracks the unnatural stillness of her face. "Ellen wants nothing to do with me."

Okay, I can work with this. "Are you sure?" I ask. "I know her pretty well, and I've never seen her ignore *any-one* as hard as she's ignoring you." Wait, that didn't come out right.

She blanches. "That's, uh, good to know."

"What I mean," I say quickly, "is that she must have some pretty strong feelings to act that way." For no reason at all, I think of Max. *Focus, Lily!*

"You don't understand. Twenty years ago, I left Clark-town without even saying goodbye. At the time, I felt stuck, like I had to get out of this town or I'd end up stuck here for the rest of my life, but I broke Ellen's heart, and she never forgave me for it. Your mother didn't either."

"The important thing is that you're back now," I say, "and I think my mom, at least, has forgiven you. Now we just have to work on my auntie Li." I drop my voice although everyone else is crowding the buffet table and can't possibly overhear. "Look, no one wants to do more touristy stuff. We all want to go back to our rooms and watch free cable or play games." Except for Tina, who *explicitly* said the fish tossing was one of her favorite things ever. I squash down my guilt and continue. "Why don't you send the kids to their rooms after lunch, tell my auntie Li you need to talk, and go over to the hotel lounge to figure things out?"

Her face brightens. "Do you think that will work?"

"I know it will," I say confidently. *It had better work.* Because I have twenty minutes and counting to eat lunch in record time, set up my auntie and my dance teacher, give Tina the slip, change into my vampire cosplay outfit, and book it to Comic Con.

Vivienne's back straightens as Auntie Li enters the restaurant. "It's worth a shot!"

It certainly is.

EIGHTEEN

HEART POUNDING, I RACE ALONG busy Pike Street, not caring that people are staring at a twelve-year-old in the outfit that Drusilla, a vampire, wore on *Buffy*, Season 2, Episode 21 (a lacy red tank top that I'm freezing in and a long maroon velvet skirt that I'm sweating in—thanks, Kelli).

At last I come to a panting halt in front of the convention center. At long last! I really didn't think I was going to make it because I had to eat a whole plate of food to keep Tina from getting suspicious, and I'm not sure that it worked anyway. She had a funny look on her face when I didn't go back for a second plate. A sour taste fills my mouth, and it's not the tempura shrimp I speed-ate.

I slam the door on my conscience. The important thing is that I'm here, and just in time to see the actors who played Faith and Spike.

Still out of breath, I step up to the ticket taker and hand her my ticket, but she doesn't take it.

Instead, she looks me up and down. "How old are you?" she asks suspiciously.

"Uh . . ." My heart starts banging against my chest. What's the right answer? Eighteen? Twenty-one? Scared to overshoot, I blurt out the truth. "Twelve."

"Sorry, kid. Anyone under the age of thirteen has to be accompanied by an adult."

You've got to be kidding me. If I had just tacked on one measly year, she would have let me in?

She's waving me away before it finally sinks in. I'm going to miss Comic Con.

Frantically, I text my friends.

> Here now but they won't let me in without an adult! What should I do?

Lauren will logic them into letting me in or Kelli will cry and be all dramatic. They won't let me miss Comic Con. My stomach knots as I wait for a response.

Ten minutes pass with my eyes glued to my tablet, but there's nothing. That's when I remember something that makes my whole body go cold. There's no cell phone reception inside the convention center. My friends can't help me. They might even think I've abandoned them for no reason. Suddenly, it feels as if I've been stabbed through the heart with one of the plastic stakes in my backpack.

Forlornly, I pop my vampire teeth out of my mouth and put on a hoodie from my backpack. Then I start to trudge back to the hotel. At least there's one good thing that came out of all my scheming—Auntie Li and Vivienne. My last glimpse of them (before I dashed out of the restaurant to change into my vampire outfit) was of them talking intensely with their heads close together—so there's that at least. And almost everyone was delighted by the reprieve from more tourist activities.

Except for Tina. A pang of guilt hits me. Maybe I can fix things by offering to hang out now. But I remember her hard expression when I turned down her suggestion to go watch the fish tossing on our own. And since she's my roommate, she's going to notice that I'm not watching TV in our hotel room like I said I would be.

No, I've ruined my friendship with Tina . . . and it was all for nothing.

My head droops and I stare at the cracks in the sidewalk, not caring that my skirt is dragging on the ground. Come to think of it, I don't think I can handle going back to the hotel to face Tina.

"Hey, let's not crash into each other again," a familiar voice says.

I look up to see Max. "What are you doing here?" My voice is listless, and I can't even work up the energy to accuse him of stalking me. Besides, it's obvious why he's here. Max has been moping in dance practice all week because the rest of us were going to spend a weekend in Seattle and see a dance performance. He must have convinced his parents to bring him to the city for the show.

The amusement in his eyes fades. "What's wrong?"

Sympathy from him is the last straw. I burst into tears.

Alarm flashes across his face. "I'm just here to catch the Fenghuang dance performance tonight! I swear! I'm not trying to spy on you or anything!"

"I know." I dab my wet eyes with the sleeve of my hoodie. "It's just that I've made a mess of *everything*. I can't go to Comic Con because I'm only twelve, and I can't go back to the hotel because Tina is mad at me for blowing *her* off." I hiccup on a sob. "I have nowhere to go!"

He stares at me in silence for a moment. "Want to hang out?" he asks finally. "My mom is doing some shopping, and she said I could go to the arcade and play some games. I was on my way there."

"No thanks." I don't need a pity hang with Max.

"Okay." An awkward silence stretches between us, but he doesn't make any move to leave. "How about we go to Pacific Place and get a cupcake, then? A cupcake always makes *me* feel better when I've alienated my friends and have nowhere to go." Then he peers at me. "Too soon?"

My mouth turns up in a reluctant smile. "Too soon

to make fun of my utter despair? Why would you think that?"

"Well, I think the last time I made fun of your"—he pauses to make air quotes—"'utter despair,' it was last year during our science creature habitat presentations when my rat escaped his habitat and chewed up the bamboo in your panda habitat. If I remember correctly, you didn't respond well when I pointed out that it's not like your panda stuffie was going to starve to death."

Lauren, Kelli, and I made that panda habitat together, and Kelli even made us matching panda costumes to wear to school on the day of the presentation. Longing washes over me. Have they even noticed that I'm not at Comic Con?

"Whatever," I say to Max with a shrug. "It was just a presentation."

"Who are you and what have you done with Lily?" he demands. "Quick. Prove you're Lily and answer this question. What was the first thing you ever said to me?"

"How am I supposed to remember that? It was over two years ago in fifth grade." But the truth is, I remember it perfectly. I sigh. "I said, 'Max Zhang, you're about to get the fight of your life.'"

"Best reading challenge ever," he says nostalgically. "We were an unbeatable team after I showed you the errors of your ways."

"Ha! Our class definitely didn't need your monosyllabic book summaries to win. What was your summary of *Goodnight Moon* again? Oh, right—kid says goodnight to stuff in his room."

"*There* she is," he says, satisfaction ringing in his voice. "For the record, I never actually read or summarized *Goodnight Moon* for the challenge, and if I had, 'goodnight' is technically *two* syllables. Oh, and summaries are actually *supposed* to be short. Maybe that's why Ms. Morrison didn't accept your five-page, point-by-point comparison of the novel, the movie, and the graphic novel versions of *A Wrinkle in Time*."

I can't believe he remembers that "summary." For some reason, my spirits lift. "You know," I announce suddenly, "a cupcake *does* sound good." After all, I did skip the dessert table at the lunch buffet.

He doesn't seem thrown by my sudden change of mind. "Apparently, cupcakes have a mellowing effect on you. Noted."

I glare at him. "You'll see how 'mellow' I get if we keep standing around talking about cupcakes and not actually eating them."

"I know just the place." Then his eyes drift to my outfit. "By the way, what is—"

"Don't ask." I hike my skirt up and tuck the extra material into the waistband. I'm supposed to bring the outfit back to Kelli on Monday, so I'd better not ruin it by letting the hem drag on the dirty street or she might never speak to me again. "Okay, let's go."

It must have cost him a huge effort not to ask more questions, but he doesn't say a word about my outfit as we walk toward Pacific Place.

Relenting, I say, "Kelli made our cosplay outfits. I'm supposed to be Drusilla, a vampire from *Buffy*. Kelli is Willow—she's a witch, and Lauren is Kendra—a slayer. On the show, Drusilla is the enemy, but in our alternate universe version, we're all friends." I pause. "That was our theme. 'Unlikely friends.' Except I'm not with them right now, so they're short one vampire friend."

"I'm sure they'll understand. I've seen the three of you together, and I've seen you with Tina too." His voice is sympathetic. "You've got good friends. It will be okay."

Against all odds, I feel a bit better. "Thanks."

"So . . . you're really into all this fantasy stuff, huh? *Buffy* and Comic Con and all that."

It's an obvious attempt to change the subject and distract me from my friend troubles, but I'm touched by the effort. "I guess so."

"And your Medusa film was so cool!" His voice brims with enthusiasm.

I come to a screeching halt and stare at him in shock. "How do you know about that?"

Red sweeps over his face. "I, uh, might have watched it on Mr. Orwell's computer when we were trying to upload *Of Mice and Mazes* on the school website. It turns out there's a weird issue with a firewall that's keeping us from uploading my film. . . . Anyway, you don't need to hear all that." His face turns even brighter. "What I'm trying to say is that your film was way better than mine."

I should say something polite like, *No, yours was better*. But it wouldn't be true. And Max and I have never bothered with politeness anyway. "It's what I want to do," I say instead. "Make films, I mean."

The redness starts to fade from his face. "That makes sense. You're good at it."

We reach Pacific Place then, and our pace picks up as we catch sight of the cupcake stand. All other topics are forgotten while we choose the flavors we want.

After a heated debate (and much sighing from the teenager waiting for us to make up our minds), we decide to split a chocolate and a salted caramel cupcake. Max treats me, and we bring the cupcakes to a table in the mall.

I take a delicious sweet and salty bite. Mmm. First the dumplings, and now this. If Max doesn't end up as a dancer, he has a career ahead of him as a food guide. If there is such a thing. Reminded of our earlier conversation, I ask, "What about you? You're such an amazing dancer. Is that what you want to do?"

He chews for a few seconds without answering. At last he says, "Yes. But it's complicated."

I think back to his mother talking about the academic prep focus at his Chinese school in Seattle. "Your parents?" I ask sympathetically.

"Yeah." He sighs. "It's not like they've ever said I *couldn't* do dance. It's just that . . ." He trails off.

"They wouldn't understand?" I finish for him.

He nods. "That's it exactly."

"I get it. It's the same with my parents about me and film."

Max lifts up his half of the salted caramel cupcake and bumps mine with it. "A toast," he says, "to following our dreams."

"I'll eat to that."

As we finish our cupcakes, we talk about our future careers—me as a filmmaker of fantastical movies and Max as a dancer performing all over the world.

As I'm licking the last crumbs from my lips, Max clears his throat.

"What? Do I have something on my face?" I ask.

"No." His gaze shifts around awkwardly. "I just . . . there's something I want to show you when we get back to Clarktown."

My eyebrows rise. "Okay. Can you give me a hint?"

"It's better if I show you. Can you come somewhere with me after dance practice on Monday?"

"Sure, but you're acting super sketchy. What's this all about?"

Max just smiles mysteriously. "You'll see."

NINETEEN

"I CAN'T BELIEVE YOU MISSED Comic Con!" Kelli says for the millionth time as we approach the community center art room. I have an Art Club contact in Joanne, a high schooler who used to go to Hong Chinese Academy, and she has agreed to hook us up with a last-minute prop for our film.

"Kelli, stop," Lauren says. "Lily already feels bad enough about it."

"Just tell me that it was horrible and that James Marsters and Eliza Dushku were stuck-up."

"Actually, they were really nice—" Kelli begins.

Lauren interrupts her. "You didn't miss a thing."

"Liar." But a reluctant smile tugs at my mouth.

"Lauren's right." Kelli nods. "It was the worst one I've ever been to."

I roll my eyes. "It was the *only* Comic Con you've ever been to."

"Well, it was a terrible Comic Con," Kelli says staunchly.

Unfortunately, that's when Stacey, head of the Star Trek Club (dressed in her full Starfleet officer outfit), comes around the corner. She glares at Kelli. "It was *not* terrible. I saw Sonequa Martin-Green from *Star Trek: Discovery* there!"

Kelli turns red, and I say quickly, "She didn't mean it, Stacey. My friends were just trying to make me feel better because I missed out on Comic Con over the weekend."

"Oh," Stacey says sympathetically. "I'm sorry you missed it, especially since it was—"

"So great." I sigh. "Yeah, I'm getting that."

Stacey clears her throat. "Well, I have to go. The United Federation of Planets has an arbitration meeting scheduled for today." She hurries off as my friends stare after her.

"I'm sorry," Lauren says, "but did she say 'United Federation of Planets arbitration meeting' just now?"

"Yeah," I reply. "Star Trek Club is the place to go if you have a problem at the community center."

Kelli shakes her head as if to clear it. "This place is so weird."

"I don't see what's so weird about it." My voice is sharp. Our community center can't be the only one where the Star Trek Club handles disagreements. Well, okay, maybe we are, but that doesn't make us *weird*.

With more force than necessary, I shove open the art room door.

Joanne looks up from a worktable scattered with paintbrushes and bits of plaster and wire as we enter. "Hello, there! You have great timing. I just finished." She smiles and holds up a thing of absolute beauty. "Is this what you had in mind? A larger-than-life, bloodred heart made out of modeling clay?"

"Ooh, that's perfect!" I say. The original screenplay called for Kelli just to stake Lincoln in the heart, but I decided that we needed something with more of a visual punch. So now she's going to first pull a fake heart out of his bloody chest and *then* stake it, fake blood flying everywhere. It's going to be *so* much fun. "Do you mind if I record you while you tell us how you made it?" I dig my tablet out from my backpack. "In case we do a 'making of the movie' cut?"

"I guess I don't mind." She eyes me thoughtfully. "You know, I can do more than just this. I paint scenery all the time in case you need backdrops."

"That's okay." I aim my tablet at Joanne. "We don't need any backdrops. The whole movie takes place in a school, so the empty rooms and hallways in the community center are fine."

"Oh, are you using the Chinese school classrooms, then?"

My face goes hot as I zoom in on Joanne's face. No

way are we going to film in the Chinese school class-rooms—not unless I want my mom to catch me. It's risky enough to be filming in the community center. My body scrunches up like I can make myself invisible before I remember that I'm not technically doing anything wrong. Hopefully, that's how Mom will see it if she finds out that I'm late to dance practice every day because I'm filming a video for the Clarktown's Got Talent competition. "No, the desks are too small." Changing the subject, I say, "Tell me about the materials you used to make the heart."

At dance rehearsal, I can tell right away that Tina has decided to ignore me. A lump of sadness forms in my throat as I look across the stage, where she's practicing the fan dance with the others and determinedly not looking at me.

"Go talk to her!" Max says, grunting from my weight.

Carefully balancing on his thighs, I say, "I don't think that's a good idea."

Tina caught me sneaking back into our hotel room in full Drusilla vampire getup. I had absolutely no excuse prepared and just stammered something about trying a new look. She scanned me from head to toe and very seriously asked me if I had joined a cult. If I'd been thinking clearly, I would have said "Yes."

Because I honestly think joining a cult would have

been better than the truth—that I had ditched Tina and lied about it to spend time with my other friends but ended up hanging out with Max for two hours instead of going to the darned fish market with her like she had wanted. And that *I* was responsible for the cancellation of the fish market trip in the first place. *Yeah, a cult would have definitely been better.* But I didn't tell her the truth, and it was clear that I was keeping something from her . . . so we didn't talk much after that.

I move my arms to the left and then to the right in time to the drumbeat. When I'm holding the head, it will seem like the lion is looking from side to side. "What is it that you want to show me after dance practice again?" I ask, hopping onto the ground and switching places with him. Except for the part where I need to balance on him, it's better for him to be the head of the lion—since he actually knows what he's doing and all.

"Just wait. But I think you'll like it." Max moves fluidly into the steps, and I know they're a lot simpler and slower than he's capable of, but it's still kicking my tail. Pun intended.

Vivienne is bouncing around the stage, saying "Good! Good!" and smiling at everyone.

I'm glad *someone* (or two someones) enjoyed our field trip. Auntie Li was just as giddy as Vivienne when I saw them together at the Fenghuang performance, so I guess their talk went well. *Good.* Because the weekend was a total bust for me. Although I did have fun with Max . . .

When class is over, I pull Daniel aside and say, "Can you stay at the center and play some *Minecraft* with Ms. Leticia? I've got to do something with Max, and then I'll come pick you up in an hour, okay?"

"Sure!" Daniel says, as I knew he would. The thought of an extra hour of *Minecraft* even distracted him from asking what I'm doing with Max.

Tina looks over from where she's talking with Julia, and for a moment, it looks like she's going to say something to me.

I hold my breath in hope, but then she turns away.

My heart plummets, but I lift my chin and follow Max out of the auditorium. Whatever his surprise is—it had better be amazing to make up for this crummy day.

"Why are we at your parents' office?" I ask skeptically. This is a *major* letdown after all of Max's mysterious buildup. Their office is only about five blocks away from the school in a plain brick downtown building, and it's sandwiched between a laser surgery place and a laundromat in what I think used to be an accountants' office.

"The thing I want to show you is in there," he says calmly.

I peer into the window, but it's all dark inside and I can't see much. "Is it even open?"

"My parents spend most of their time in their Seattle

office," he explains, "but I have a key." He pulls out a key ring from his backpack and opens the door. "Coming?"

I shrug and follow him inside. Maybe he stashed the robot Minotaur he used for *Of Mice and Mazes* here.

Max flicks on the lights, revealing a few big industrial-looking desks, old metal filing cabinets, and blue carpet that looks as old as the one at the community center (and might be the same carpet, in fact). It's safe to say that I'm underwhelmed by Max's big surprise so far.

He goes to one of the ancient filing cabinets and pulls out the second drawer from the top. "Here," he says, removing a long cardboard tube. "Take a look at this."

"What is it?" My interest picks up. "A treasure map?"

He gives me an exasperated glance. "I know you want to be a filmmaker and have watched a lot of adventure movies, but why is 'treasure map' *always* your go-to response?"

"Is not!" I say indignantly.

"Oh yeah?" he counters. "When Daniel said he'd made something in *Minecraft*, what did you say?"

"Why *wouldn't* he make a treasure map? And the adventure he made did actually have one."

"Uh huh," he says. "And last weekend, when you told me that all your birthdays have a theme, and I asked what this year's was going to be . . ."

"I said a treasure *hunt*. Which isn't the same as a treasure *map*."

He grins. "Fine! But this isn't a treasure map. It's even better."

"That's a bold claim, Max Zhang." I cross my arms, but I'm smiling. If I can make up with my archenemy, then maybe I can make up with Tina, who I've known forever. The tight pain in my chest loosens a bit.

He carries the tube over to one of the big desks and slides out a roll of paper. Then, with a dramatic flourish, he unrolls it. "Ta-da!"

A drawing of a building. Really tall. Lots of glass. Lots of metal. Super new. A sick feeling spreads through me from the pit of my stomach. Shakily, I ask, "What *is* this?" I have a suspicion that I don't want to hear the answer.

Max's grin fades. "It's the blueprint of the building my parents want to build on the community center site."

That's what I was afraid of. My most nightmarish imagining was that the Zhangs would build a fancy new community center with rents so high that no one could afford it. But this? This is much worse. It's not even a community center. It's a high-rise office building. A choked gagging sound bursts out of me.

Max seems puzzled by my reaction. "Lily, what's wrong? I wanted to show you that my parents aren't trying to ruin anything. They're going to make it better."

"You can't be serious!" I stare at him in disbelief. "How is tearing down the center and putting up a mega-rich yuppie building *better*?"

"Oh!" He does a facepalm. "I should have explained!" He taps the blueprint, pointing out a space carved out between the fitness center and a coffee shop. It's labeled "HCA." Eagerly, he says, "It's for your Chinese school! My parents will give your parents a big discount, and your school will have new classrooms and the best tech—just like the Chinese school I go to in Seattle. Actually . . ." He flushes a little. "The plan is for me to go to your school once it moves into the new building. Won't that be cool?"

How clueless can he get? "Do you really think you can bribe us with a fancy school? No way will my family go for this!" I'm so furious that I wouldn't be surprised if there were literal steam coming out of my ears.

"Whoa!" He holds up his hands. "Calm down, Lily! I don't think you understand. My parents get to build something nice for Clarktown, your family gets a brand-new school, and I get to be at Chinese school with you . . . all of you."

"Who wants to be like your stupid, high-octane school in the city, anyway! And who wants you at *our* Chinese school?"

Hurt steals over his face, and he mutters, "It was just a thought."

I feel a pang of guilt, but then I think about all those kids at school upset about losing the center. Faintness creeps over me, and I actually have to grip the edge of the desk for support. What about the Amharic language school, the preschool, the Fencing Team, the senior Zumba classes, and . . . ? "Your parents didn't make space for the other community groups," I say flatly. "What's going to happen to them?"

"Oh." He looks down, avoiding my eyes. "I don't . . . I guess I didn't think of that."

Right. Because he was too busy getting a new Chinese school for himself in Clarktown. But—why does he care, anyway? Max hates the Chinese school he goes to in Seattle, so why does he want to go to ours? I peer at him uneasily.

He's tracing a space on the blueprint with one finger but doesn't seem to be aware of what he's doing. Automatically, I glance at the spot he's tracing—and my heart stops cold. "What's that next to the smoothie shop?"

He snatches his finger off the blueprint and steps in front of me. "Nothing."

Ducking under his arm, I get close to the blueprint and squint at the spot he was tracing. "Dance studio?" My voice goes high. "Are you kidding? A dance studio?" Glaring at him, I say, "This is all so you can keep working with Vivienne without going behind your parents' back! Argh! It makes sense now!"

"You're wrong!" His voice is filled with desperation. "Yes, I get something out of it too, but my parents are really trying to do a good thing for Clarktown!"

"No, Max." A deadly anger is sweeping through me. "Your family is destroying our community center, and you don't see how wrong it is!"

His face hardens. "You're the one who doesn't understand!"

I stumble away from him, unable to believe that I actually trusted him—that we were starting to be friends. "This is all a selfish plan to get what *you* really want. You don't care about anyone else." I search my brain frantically for the worst possible thing to say. Something so devastating that it will haunt him for the rest of his life, but all I can come up with is this: "I'm changing the name of my film's villain back to Maxistopheles Maxiavelli!"

But Max stares at me like he's lost his pet rat *and* his last friend on earth.

TWENTY

"NO, WE CAN'T CHANGE THE villain's name back to Max-istopheles Maxiavelli," Lauren says calmly.

"Why not?" I demand as I finish my video of the outside of the community center. With a little editing, I can make it look like the front of a high school. It's time I recommit to this film, and the first step is remaking the demon businessman villain into Max's image. Okay, maybe I don't quite have my priorities straight. . . .

Kelli answers me as I open the side door to the community center. "For one thing," she says, flicking her hair over one shoulder, "Tim quit the film. So we're out one villain."

"What?!" I glance down our usual hallway/film set. There's Suzie in her cheerleader/vampire costume, running lines with Lincoln. But . . . "Where's the rest of the cast?"

"Tim refused to sing, Marissa made it onto the basketball team at school, and Chelsea got into a fight with Lincoln because he was messing around and sprayed fake blood on her favorite sneakers," Kelli explains. "So they all quit."

Lauren adds, "Now Lincoln has Marissa's lines because we combined the two best friend parts into one character. And Suzie is playing all the extras."

My head whirls. "Wait. Go back to that first thing again."

"Marissa's doing basketball—" Kelli begins.

"No. Before that."

She scratches her head for a second. "You mean the part where I said Tim quit because he won't sing? Right. About that—we voted at the end of yesterday's shoot to make the film a musical."

"Kelli!" Frustration wells up in me. "Half the cast can't sing!" That's why I nixed her musical idea right from the beginning.

She flushes. "Well, you weren't here! So you don't get a say!"

"*I* voted against it." Lauren glances at me reproachfully. "But with our director MIA, there wasn't anything I could do."

My stomach tightens. I was gone ten measly minutes. How did Kelli stage a coup in such a short time? She's always wanted to do *The Chosen One Slays Big Business on* the Hellmouth: *A Musical in Three Parts*, but I can't believe that she would stoop this low. "So, you waited until I left before saying, 'Hey, everyone, how about a musical?'"

"That's not how it happened," Kelli protests. "It was actually Lincoln's idea."

"Yeah, it was." Lauren's voice turns sour. "But Kelli agreed."

I breathe deeply and try to stay calm. Getting mad at Kelli isn't going to help, and like they both said—I wasn't here. Still, I do have a stake in this movie since I'm the director and all.

"So now we don't have a villain?" I grumble.

Kelli's flush deepens. "We actually came up with a solution for that." She unzips her backpack and pulls out a familiar-looking red lace and maroon velvet dress. "Congratulations," she says, placing the Drusilla outfit into my arms. "You've just been cast as Maxistopheles Maxiavelli or whatever you want to call the demon business . . . woman. You're going to be great!" she says brightly.

"Kelli," I say, trying hard to hold on to my patience, "we've already shot *three* whole scenes. Maybe we can do without Marissa and Chelsea, but we can't just swap villains halfway through the movie. Can't we just tell Tim that it's not going to be a musical and ask him to come back?"

Kelli's mouth sets. "That's not going to work."

"Things were said," Lauren explains.

In other words, Kelli lost her temper.

"But . . . but . . ." I sputter. *I can't sing! I can't act!*

Kelli knows all that already and judging from the desperation in her eyes, she doesn't care. "Please." She clasps her hands together.

I look to Lauren, hoping she can talk sense into Kelli, but she just says, "You already know the lines. You're perfect." It's obvious they've talked about it already and have come to an agreement.

Feeling trapped, I say, "I suppose I can write in some kind of transformation ritual that explains why the demon looks different. . . ."

"That sounds great! See, I knew you'd think of something." Kelli looks relieved. She won't look so happy when she sees the exposition-heavy dialogue I give her—we simply don't have time to film a whole new scene to explain the transformation. And if I *do* play the villain, I will definitely edit down my own lines as much as possible.

The bundle of velvet and lace feels heavy in my arms. "I still have to leave filming early today to pick up Daniel from Minecraft Club."

Lauren and Kelli exchange a look, and an uneasy feeling crawls into my stomach.

"Here's the thing." Lauren takes a deep breath. "Yesterday, I came back to the center with my parents for a community meeting, and I saw Daniel playing a game with Ms. Leticia. If you have to leave filming early to take him home every day, then what was he still doing at the center?"

Oh . . . darn. My palms go damp with sweat. That was when Max was showing me the plans for the high-rise office building.

Lauren and Kelli are both watching me expectantly, but I don't know what to say. No excuse comes to mind. Panic sets in, and my throat feels tight from the lies I've been telling my friends.

"Do you even want to make this film anymore?" Kelli asks. She doesn't sound mad—just confused.

"Of course I do! This film is super important to me!" Less important now that it's a musical, but one look at Kelli makes me decide to keep that thought to myself. It's not like I have a death wish. "Look, I'll play the part of the villain." What else can I do?

Kelli smiles with relief. "Thank you."

Suzie and Lincoln are getting louder and louder, and Suzie yells, "That's my line! Stop stealing my lines!"

Kelli whips around. "Hey, you had better not mess up this scene again!"

While her back is turned, Lauren whispers to me, "Can you stay the whole time today? If you're not here, Kelli might turn our movie into something worse than a musical."

I agree reluctantly without saying what I'm really thinking—that there could be only one thing worse than being cast, against my will, as a singing villain in a hijacked version of the screenplay I wrote.

And that would be starring in the movie of my life.

A few days later, I'm panting and running down the halls of Clarktown Community Center, stumbling over my long skirt and getting tangled in the heavy folds of velvet. With all the running I've been doing in this outfit lately, you'd think I'd have figured out how to manage this unnecessary amount of fabric. I'm extra, *super* late this time. Even Kelli, amazing as she is, struggled to deliver her new lines about witnessing the Rites of Hespa that allowed the demon to transform into a new body, which (small and slight as it might seem) was actually mightier if less talkative. . . . Fine, it wasn't exactly my best work. But Kelli spouting lengthy and hastily written exposition is still better than giving myself any more lines than strictly necessary. If I'd had any hope of suddenly becoming a decent actor in the five years since I played the Tin Girl in *The Wizard of Clarktown* . . . well, let's just say those hopes have died a fiery death.

If it weren't for Max, I'd almost prefer dance practice to filming. But Vivienne refused to let me switch back to being a fan dancer, so I'm stuck working with that traitor Max on the lion dance. Obviously, I'm ignoring him as much as I can . . . even though he keeps giving me pathetic puppy-dog looks. Not that I feel bad for him. Not one tiny bit. Nope. Nothing. My heart is as hard as one of Medusa's stone human victims. *Stone, you hear?*

I slow as I pass the bathroom. Do I have time to change into the lion-dance costume bouncing in my backpack? No. If I change now, I'll just have to change back into the demon businesswoman costume later.

Because my life really, really sucks.

It was clearly not my brightest move when I pretended that I needed to go to the bathroom. *They're going to notice when you don't come back*, a little voice whispers. Sweat pricks the back of my neck. *Shut up*, I tell the voice. *I was desperate and didn't have any other ideas.*

The voice has a response to that too. *Then you should have just told them the truth.* This time, I don't tell it to shut up. First, because it's weird to keep talking to the voice inside my head, but—more important—the voice, even if it's just a figment of my imagination, is right. I do need to come clean to my friends.

Was it my imagination, or did Lauren and Kelli look after me suspiciously when I announced *way* too loudly (in retrospect) that I had to go to the bathroom, picked up my backpack, and ran down the hall? *Yeah, not my imagination.* They know I'm up to something—they just don't know what it is.

But I don't have time to worry about my friends right

now. I gather up the skirt and sprint the rest of the way to the auditorium. I don't know how many points I've scored with Vivienne for orchestrating the setup with Auntie Li, but I have a feeling I'm going to need them all for being twenty minutes late to practice.

When I get there at last, I run through the doors and try to catch my breath and gasp out an apology at the same time. "Sorry . . . for being . . . late," I wheeze.

Max's eyes widen and he falters in midstep. After one glance, Daniel looks away and keeps practicing his fan sweeps. He's been furious with me over the way I've been giving Max the cold shoulder, so Daniel has been giving me the same treatment.

Tina's fan thuds to the floor, and she doesn't even pick it up; she just stares at me, stock-still and pale.

My heart plummets in sudden memory. *She saw me in this outfit before.* It was when I came back to the hotel after sneaking away to go to Comic Con. How could I have forgotten? What is she thinking? And—is she going to rat me out? But Tina stays silent, just watching me with no expression on her face.

"'Late' is an understatement at this point." Vivienne punctuates each word with a flutter of her fan. "And *what* are you wearing?"

I gulp and frantically try to think of an explanation, but Vivienne just shakes her head and points backstage, where we've been changing since we started practicing in costume a few days ago. "Just get dressed."

"I'll help," Tina says. "The sash is tricky."

The sash *is* tricky—but not as tricky as the conversation I suspect we're about to have. Stomach clenched, I follow her backstage and pull out the white satin pants and matching wide-sleeved tunic with the red and gold embroidered sash. "Thanks for helping me," I mumble as I pull the tunic over the red lace top.

Without waiting for me to put on the pants, Tina starts tying the sash so the long ends fall just right. "I saw you in this weird goth outfit last weekend!" she whispers furiously. "You're always late to dance, have no time to hang out, and now you're keeping secrets from me?"

A hard lump rises up in my throat. I'm sick of lying to all my friends. It's time to confess. "Tina—" I begin.

And then a voice slices through the peaceful melody of Chinese classical music. "Where is Lily? I need to talk to her now!"

It's Mom. Ice-cold shivers cascade down my body. *And she sounds like she's out for blood.*

TWENTY-ONE

"LILY IS GETTING DRESSED," VIVIENNE says, sounding surprised.

"What is the Zhang boy doing here?" Mom's voice rises. "Hong Li Hua, you are in *so* much trouble!"

Sweat makes my armpits damp. My full name in Chinese is a *very bad* sign. But why is Max *my* fault?

Another voice rings through the auditorium. "Zhang Min Zhe! Why are you here and not at your Chinese school?" *Max's mom is here too?*

Rapid footsteps coming closer indicate that our mothers are coming onto the stage.

"Mom, I can explain!" Max sounds totally scared. Reluctant sympathy creeps through me. I know exactly how he feels.

Tina and I exchange wide-eyed looks. Then, apparently remembering that *she* doesn't have anything to hide, she steps away from me. "You'd better go out there." Her voice is almost kind.

I take a deep breath and prepare to face the music. I'm not sure what's happening, but my mom and Max's mom, both furious, is terrifying. Heart hammering madly, I go out onto the stage. Everyone is staring at me except for Max's mom, who's saying something to him in a low, but clearly angry, tone. He looks as miserable as I feel.

Mom glares at me. "I couldn't believe it when Ms. Zhang called me to tell me that she found your necklace in their office! Do you know how embarrassed I am?" Dangling from her hand is the Symbol of Anyanka pendant. The one Ms. Zhang saw me wearing before.

Hot panic rises into my throat. It must have come off when Max took me to his parents' office. *That's why my mom and his are here.* They came here to confront me, not knowing Max would be here too. Despite everything, I feel sorry for him. His mother is going to be furious to find out that he showed me the plans for the high-rise.

My mother hands me the pendant. Then, in a deathly quiet voice, she asks, "Did you trespass onto the Zhangs' property, Lily?"

It feels like a thousand eels are slithering in my stomach as I take the necklace. I want to tell her the truth, but it would mean ratting on Max. I look at my feet as I try to think of something to say that won't get him in trouble, but my throat is dry and my mind is blank.

"She didn't trespass!" Max says. "I took her to my parents' office!"

My head snaps up. Did Max just take a hit for me?

His eyes meet mine, but before either of us can say anything, a loud gasp comes from the open auditorium doors.

Oh, darn. I know that gasp. *Kelli.* Slowly, I turn to the auditorium doors, dread coiling in my stomach.

Lauren is staring at me in open shock, and Kelli has a hand clapped over her mouth. They start walking toward us, and it's not a long aisle, so I have probably ten seconds to figure out how to explain this to them. . . .

Of course, my mind is still blank when they reach the steps to the stage. "Did Max just say you went with him to his parents' office?" Lauren asks.

"And why are you in that costume?" Kelli asks.

I look down at my friends' confused faces and then at the white wide-sleeved tunic and the embroidered slash hanging over the maroon velvet skirt Kelli made for me. My skin goes clammy. *Will she believe this is an upgrade of my demon businesswoman costume?*

Kelli's gaze lands on Max. "Lily, what's going on? What is Max doing here?"

"Do you have something against my son?" Ms. Zhang's voice is cold.

Kelli flushes and doesn't seem to know what to say, but Lauren speaks up. "We have nothing against Max."

She glances at me. "We're just wondering why our friend would go to your office with him."

Ms. Zhang's hard expression melts into confusion. "Actually, I'm wondering that too." She turns to Max. "Why would you take Lily to our office and not tell us?"

Telling his mother that I didn't break into their office is one thing, but confessing to what we were doing there is a totally different thing.

But Max looks her right in the eyes. "I wanted to show Lily your plans for the community center."

No way! He actually went there.

Oddly, Ms. Zhang doesn't even look mad. "I suppose that news is out now." She turns to Mom with a wry smile. "I meant it as a surprise, but I might as well let you all know about our plans for this site."

My gut tightens in horror. Max was right. His parents actually think they're doing a good thing for Clarktown. *Stop!* I want to scream. *This is not going to go the way you think it will!*

I clutch Anyanka's pendant in my hand, and its sharp edges dig into my palm. I don't think of Max's mom as the enemy anymore. She's like Anya, whose hurt and betrayal turned her into a vengeance demon. Or Drusilla, whose dress I'm wearing. She trusted the wrong vampire and got bitten. They're villains only if you don't know their stories, and remembering Ms. Zhang's eager awkwardness around my mother and the excited way she loaded me with food—I think I do know a little of her story. She wants friends for Max . . . and for herself. My heart aches for her.

Ms. Zhang, her eyes shining with excitement, announces, "We're planning to build a mixed-use office high-rise!" She doesn't seem to notice the dead silence that greets her announcement. "It will be beautiful! Modern, new, with all the latest technology!"

Kelli groans, and Lauren just shakes her head. Tina makes a choking noise. Daniel's eyes dart around the room like he's scoping out a hiding place to ride out the storm. Vivienne's eyes flutter closed, and I wonder if she's having one of her dramatic fainting fits, but her eyes open again, sharp and focused. The other kids look confused. Max is as pale as a ghost.

The silent treatment I gave Max all week stabs at my conscience, and my stomach cramps with sympathy and fear.

"Oh?" Mom asks flatly.

That seems to pierce Ms. Zhang's enthusiasm, but then she brightens up again. "I forgot to tell you the best part! Don't worry, Xiaozhang," she says, "your school will get a prime spot at a very reasonable rent. The space will be so much better than what you have now. . . ." Her voice finally trails off as she looks at my mother's stony face.

Frostily, my mother says, "Thank you for your

generous offer, Ms. Zhang—"

"Elizabeth," Ms. Zhang says in a small voice. "Call me Elizabeth."

Mom forges ahead as if Ms. Zhang hadn't spoken. "But I must refuse." She folds her arms across her chest. "I could not possibly move into your building, knowing that other organizations will lose their home."

Ms. Zhang's face turns as red as a tomato, and she looks around the room, seeming to take in the chilly expressions and silence.

"In any case, the center isn't yours yet," Mom says. "And as I told you, our fundraiser is going to bring in the money necessary for the Clarktown Community Nonprofit to buy the center."

Pride in my mom makes my chest puff out. But I deflate a bit when she says, "Again, I apologize for my daughter trespassing on your property. It won't happen again."

Still red in the face, Ms. Zhang says faintly, "No apologies necessary." She glances at Max, whose head is hanging down. "And I apologize for my son intruding on your dance performance. That won't happen again either."

Max raises startled eyes. "Mom, you can't do that! No one minds me being here."

Mom opens her mouth, but Vivienne interrupts her. "That's absolutely right," she says firmly. "We couldn't do this performance without Max."

Mom glowers at Vivienne. "You and I need to have a talk about admitting students who don't even attend our school."

"That won't be necessary," Ms. Zhang says. "Please send me an invoice, and I'll pay for the dance classes he's attended." Her eyes are brimming with hurt disbelief, like she can't understand how she went wrong. She places a hand on Max's shoulder. "We're leaving now, and I can promise that my son won't bother you anymore."

Max and I look at each other in shock. *This can't be happening.* "Wait!" I call out. "Max is a really good dancer, and this is his dream!"

A small, sad smile sneaks over his face.

Lauren and Kelli look at me with astonished expressions, but I can't worry about what they're thinking.

Then a hand slips into mine. Tina has come to my side. Surprised gratitude rushes into me, and I squeeze her hand. She squeezes back.

"Lily is right." Daniel walks over to stand next to me. He doesn't hold my hand, but he gives me a nod. "We need Max."

For a moment, I think it could be okay. Tina is my friend again, Daniel is speaking to me, and Max, my former archenemy, stood up for me. Surely, his mother will see that he belongs with us. I remember how excited Ms. Zhang was when she thought I was Max's friend. She just wants what's best for him. *This can't end with Max leaving.*

"I'm sorry," Ms. Zhang says stiffly, "but we won't stay where we're not wanted." Then she drags him from the room.

My last sight of Max is of his hunched shoulders and dejected hang of his head.

TWENTY-TWO

MOM IS THE FIRST ONE to break the stunned silence after the Zhangs' dramatic exit. "If you'll excuse me," she says, "I have an emergency meeting to call." She means Dad, Lauren's parents, the Morenos, and every adult who has a stake in the community center. In other words, half the town is about to descend on the community center. Mom hurries out, and her footsteps echo down the hall.

I expect Lauren, who lives for community meetings, to be hot on Mom's heels, but she and Kelli come up the steps and start whispering together in a corner of the stage. My heart beats faster. *What does this mean?*

"How are we going to do our dance without Max?" Daniel asks in a small voice. "We don't have a lion without him."

My brother is right. Max was always the better half of our lion, but it's not just his dance skills that we need. It was the energy and fun he brought to every practice and how he was always willing to help everyone out. "I don't know." Sadness seeps into me. I really thought his mom would let him stay.

"Children," Vivienne calls, "continue with practice." She looks stunned as she grabs her phone and retreats to the other side of the stage, texting furiously as she goes. Probably filling in Auntie Li.

Daniel walks over to the other fan dancers, but Tina stays by my side. "You'd better go talk to your friends." Her face is glum.

"You're right." Her hand starts to slide out of mine, but I hold on. "That means you too."

"Really?" The way her face lights up cuts me right to the heart.

It was wrong for me to take Tina for granted and not even try to include her in my other friend group. *That's all going to change now.*

"Vivienne," I call out, "can Tina and I leave for the rest of practice? We need to work on a new idea for our dance."

Tina raises an eyebrow. She thinks it's another lie, but this time, I'm telling the truth. We *do* need to change up our performance, and I need all my friends working together to pull this off.

"Go ahead." Vivienne doesn't even look up from her phone.

Lauren and Kelli stop whispering as Tina and I approach them. Lauren's eyes are wary, and Kelli's mouth is pursed in a frown. *This isn't going to be easy.*

But I have to try. "We all need to talk."

"So," I say, looking around the empty hallway, "everyone else quit the film?" We've cleared away props to make a space against the wall where the four of us are sitting. The Fencing Team has been letting us store our stuff in their practice room, but no one has the energy to clean up right now. Tina and I are next to each other, facing Kelli and Lauren.

Kelli flushes. "Maybe the musical wasn't a good idea."

That's what Lauren and I were trying to tell her, but Kelli's not the only one who made mistakes. "It wasn't totally your fault. I should have been here." Then I glance at Tina. "But I was trying to be in two places at once."

"This is why you've been late to dance rehearsals?" Tina waves a fan (for some reason, she brought her fans) at the pints of fake blood and plastic stakes littering the hall. "What is all this, anyway?"

I take a deep breath. "This," I say to Tina, "was our middle school entry in the school district's Clarktown's Got Talent video competition. It's a film called *The Chosen One Slays Big Business on the Hellmouth*."

"A musical in three parts," Kelli adds half under her breath.

Lauren scowls at her.

"Oh." Tina looks around again. "I knew you were into filmmaking, Lily. You could have told me."

"I know." Instead of thinking Tina wouldn't understand, I should have included her in my life outside of Chinese school. "I'm sorry."

"It's okay," she says, and relief fills me. "Just tell me stuff from now on."

"I will." We smile tentatively at each other, and a huge weight lifts from my heart.

"That goes for us too!" Kelli says.

I nod. "No more secrets. I promise."

Lauren looks pointedly at my embroidered sash and wide-sleeved tunic. "Are you going to explain this, then?"

"Yes," I say, but my chest is tight with regret for all the ways I've lied and let them down. How do I explain why I've been sneaking off while the film and all our dreams of the Clarktown's Got Talent video competition slowly crumbled into dust? "I'm so sorry about the film."

Lauren shakes her head. "You don't have to be sorry, Lily. We just want to understand."

"Yeah, it's just a film," Kelli says as if it's not *her* starring role we're talking about. That means a lot coming from the girl who screamed in joy for ten seconds straight when she got the role of Dorothy in *The Wizard of Clarktown* at the community center drama camp.

A lump forms in my throat to feel my friends' support

close around me like a warm blanket. Maybe it's not so hard to explain after all. "The community center is in trouble, so my mom signed us up to do a Chinese dance performance for a showcase fundraiser." There, that wasn't so bad.

"My mom did tell me about the fundraiser," Lauren says. "I should have known this is what you were up to."

"You could have told us!" Kelli says.

She's right. My gut kept telling me my friends would understand, but once I started lying, I couldn't seem to stop. "I wanted to tell you, but . . ." My chest is so tight with nerves that I can hardly breathe, but I have to just come out with it. "I told so many lies, and I was scared you would think I was a terrible person for keeping all this from you. I'm sorry. I never meant to let you down."

Kelli brushes a hand over her eyes. "That's just silly."

"You could never let us down." Lauren reaches out and hugs me.

My eyes fill with tears as I hug her back. We're both sniffling by the time we release each other and sit back down.

"Uh no," Kelli says fiercely, shaking her head. "Lily doesn't get off that easily."

My heart sinks to the ground, but a grin spreads over Kelli's face, and relief floods me. She's messing with me, but I'll totally take it if it means that things are going to be back to normal between us.

Then Kelli says, "Admit that you like Max."

The relief drains away. "No! You've got it all wrong! That's not what's happening." My face flames up. "I mean, he's not as bad as I thought, but if you're thinking . . . well, come on. We were archenemies and just became friends. Let's not jump to conclusions!" I end desperately.

"Oh, she totally likes Max," Tina says. "You should see how they dance together."

"You were dance partners?" Lauren's eyes light up.

"It's not what you think," I say primly. "He was the lion's head, and I was the tail."

"Except when Max lifted her up. Then Lily was the head."

"Lifts?!" Kelli shrieks.

I glare at Tina. "Traitor."

She ignores me and turns to Lauren and Kelli like they've all been friends for ages. "And Max *definitely* likes Lily back."

Lauren laughs. "I could have told you that back in fifth grade."

Wait. What?!

"Really?" Kelli asks indignantly. "You never told me you thought that! And you didn't even believe me a couple weeks ago when I said Lily liked Max."

Lauren shrugs. "I didn't know how Lily felt, but that

boy had it bad from the minute he met her. It was obvious."

Well, it wasn't obvious to me. It still isn't, but I can't be mad at Lauren for keeping her suspicions from me because she kept them from Kelli too. "Not a word about this to anyone at school," I threaten Kelli, "or your character in my next film will have no sense of fashion."

"You wouldn't dare."

"Try me," I say grimly. "I'm thinking khakis."

She gasps.

"As entertaining as this all is," Lauren says dryly, "don't we have a center to save?"

"Right." Gathering the folds of my velvet skirt up (and the shreds of my dignity), I wiggle into a more comfortable position on the floor. "My mom said that the showcase could raise the money we need to save the center, so I need to focus on our dance performance." I look anxiously at Kelli. "That means I won't have time for the film."

"Our film is ruined anyway!" Kelli throws her head back in her classic tragic pose.

For once, she isn't exaggerating. "Yeah," I say glumly.

Lauren shakes her head. "The video competition doesn't matter. Lily, you're right. We have to save the community center, and that's why Kelli and I"—she pauses to pin Kelli with a stern look—"will help."

"Of course." Kelli's eyes start to brighten. "With our

help, this will be the best fundraiser ever, and we'll make enough money to save the center!"

"That's great," I say, stomach churning because I'm about to pop her bubble. "But I should tell you that the acts are a little . . . um . . . unconventional. For example, the Star Trek Club doing *Hamlet*."

"That doesn't sound too bad," Lauren starts to say, but I interrupt her.

"In Klingon."

"All of it?" Lauren asks in disbelief.

"Just one scene—the one with Hamlet and the ghost," I say. "I'm told that Shakespeare works particularly well in Klingon, and you know—that scene is all about revenge and honor, so it should work well."

Lauren and Kelli stare at me with zero comprehension on their faces. I might as well be speaking Klingon myself.

"The senior Zumba class is doing a demo," Tina offers.

"Okay, that's actually awesome," I admit, "but the Quilting Club is doing their quilt-a-thon, and I'm going to be honest and say that I'm not sure how that's going to work. My dad was pretty vague when he told me about it. Then there's the Chess Club."

"Don't tell me," Lauren says. "They're going to be playing chess?"

"No. Juggling life-sized chess pieces."

Kelli drops her face into her hands.

"Right," Lauren says weakly. She glances at Tina in full costume and me in my hybrid dance/demon costume. "At least the Chinese school performance seems cool."

"It *was* cool," Tina says sadly, "but Max was our star performer. Without him, we're just a bunch of amateur kids. We haven't gotten through a rehearsal yet without Kylie doing a random somersault or someone dropping a fan." That someone was usually me when I was a fan dancer (and will be again now that there's no lion), but she's too nice to say that.

It's not fair. Tina, Daniel, and the others have been working their butts off. So has Vivienne. It would be a bummer for their work to go to waste.

"What we need," I say, mind churning, "is a little creativity." Clambering up, I hike up my skirt and start to pace.

"What is she doing?" Tina asks worriedly. She opens and closes her fans without seeming to realize what she's doing.

"You get used to it," Lauren says. "This is just how she works."

"I'm not used to it yet," Kelli grumbles.

I ignore them all and try to pace and think. Okay, *Buffy* is out, but what about a myth for the dance? Greek tragedies and epic Norse battles race through my head, but none of them seem right. We need a story about saving the community center. Something beautiful and strong . . .

Tina rises at that moment, flicking her fans open. She's gotten so good that the fans look like an extension of her arms. Like wings.

Like a phoenix rising.

My throat goes dry with wonder, and I come to a dead stop. My body tingling with excitement, I clear my throat and face my friends.

"Hong Chinese Academy is going to perform *The Phoenix and Her Community Center*."

TWENTY-THREE

—

THE NEXT DAY, VIVIENNE GASPS when I walk into the auditorium with Tina, Daniel, Lauren, and Kelli.

"Lily Hong, you're early!" She checks the clock on the wall. "Twenty minutes early."

We climb the steps to the stage, and I decide to dive right in. "We have a problem with our performance now that Max is gone."

Vivienne's face falls, and she doesn't deny this.

"But I know what we can do," I say. "Remember the story about the phoenix and her city?"

Confusion spreads over her face. "The one about the bird leaving the nest?" *Darn. Yeah, maybe I don't mention this to Dad.*

"That's not really the takeaway," I mumble.

"I don't understand," she says. "What does that story have to do with our dance?"

"Don't worry," Tina says, "she'll explain."

"With lots of details." Kelli smiles at me. I was totally willing to let her pout about losing her starring film role in the video competition, but instead, she announced that she would help with costumes, hair, and makeup for our fundraiser dance performance.

"Don't take all day, Lily!" Daniel says. He literally leaped at the chance to dance the part of the messenger goose—in that he jumped into the air with his fans flapping like he was auditioning for the part.

Lauren nudges Kelli and Daniel. "Shush. Let Lily explain."

But it's not Kelli or Daniel that makes my mouth dry and my pulse race. It's my own fears. "What we need is a story." My voice comes out more faintly than I intended, so I clear my throat and speak up. "Something that's more than a dance—a myth."

"I think I see what you're getting at," Vivienne says, "but don't you think that story is a little . . . grim? If I remember correctly, the phoenix sacrifices herself for the city of Yinchuan, even turning her heart into a drum tower in the center of the city."

"It's a story about the bird of happiness! The phoenix loves her city so much that she made herself into its protection," I say. "What's so grim about that?"

"The phoenix's sacrifice was in vain!" Vivienne's voice gets all dramatic as if she can't help getting swept up by the story. "A corrupt official plunders the city's riches and murders the phoenix! The rivers run red with the phoenix's blood when she dies at the end!"

"To be reborn!" I say, waving the minor detail of the phoenix's death aside. "Besides, endings can be changed."

"But, Lily!" Vivienne exclaims, hands fluttering. "We can't just make up a story! When I was with the Feng-huang Performers, it took months to come up with a script for the kind of thing you're talking about, and we have just three weeks! I suppose the choreography could be adapted from what we've already practiced, but we can't do this without a script for the actual story!"

I unzip my backpack and swallow the lump of nerves in my throat. "I might be able to help with that." I'm bleary-eyed from staying up half the night, but it will be worth it if this works.

Then I remember the last time I shared my work with an adult. What if Vivienne, like Mr. Orwell, thinks my script is unrealistic? Or worse, she says something kind about it being a good effort for a kid? After all, Vivienne has been in world-famous performances and has worked with professionals. I'm just a twelve-year-old kid who makes films on a tablet.

"Come on!" Kelli urges. "Show her."

"You've got this," Lauren says.

"We believe in you." Tina squeezes my arm.

"Who cares if it's no good? We just need something!"

Gee, thanks, Daniel.

But this isn't about me. This is about making our performance the best it can be. Besides . . . I'm not just a twelve-year-old amateur filmmaker. I'm the filmmaker behind *The Tragic Romance of Medusa*, *The Chosen One Slays Big Business on the Hellmouth* (which will be revived one day), *The Fairies Fight Fenrir* (a Norse myth fairy-tale mash-up), and many more. I'm ready for this.

Heart beating fast and hands shaky, I hand Vivienne a copy of my script. "It's a script for *The Phoenix and Her Community Center*."

Looking stunned, she takes it.

I hold my breath as she flips through the pages. What if she hates it?

"This actually looks pretty . . . amazing. Lily, *you* did this?"

"Yes." My voice wobbles in relief. "You really think it's okay?"

"It's better than okay! I love this dialogue. And the tension in these scenes is fantastic!" Her face turns thoughtful. "It could work. There's the main phoenix, who will be our lead dancer."

"Tina," I say at once.

Tina smiles as Lauren and Kelli cheer.

"And we have six other girls who could dance the parts of the six phoenix sisters." Vivienne's voice is getting animated.

"I'm going to dance the part of the goose!" Daniel says.

"That's perfect!" Then a crease forms on Vivienne's forehead. "But who will be the villain?"

"He's not a villain, exactly," I say, fingering Anya's pendant around my neck. I'm tired of writing straight-up bad guys. "The thief who tries to steal the phoenix's heart is more like a misguided person who thinks he's doing the right thing and doesn't mean to hurt anyone; it's just that he doesn't understand why the phoenix is so important to the people of the town."

"Well"—a voice comes from the open doors—"as long as the character isn't Maxistopheles Maxiavelli, I could take the part."

My heart leaps into my throat and does cartwheels of happiness as I turn around to see my former archenemy smirking at me from the doorway of the auditorium.

Max Zhang.

After the shrieking and hugging is over (shrieking on my part only, but hugging on both our parts), Max says, "You missed me, didn't you?"

"You're insufferable." But I'm grinning from ear to ear.

"Glad things are normal between you two," Lauren comments dryly.

Kelli is saying in a stage whisper, "I *knew* it!"

"We all knew it, Kelli," Tina says.

"Knew what?" Daniel's face scrunches up in confusion.

A smile flickers over Vivienne's face as her gaze takes in Max and me. My face goes hot, and Max is blushing too. If she says *anything* about the two of us, I swear I'll sink right through the floor.

But she just says, "Welcome back, Max! Now we have work to do!"

Kelli pipes up. "I can help with costumes and makeup!" She looks Vivienne over. "Not that you need help with any of that. Your foundation is perfectly blended, and that jumpsuit is to die for! Silk, right?"

"Yes!" Vivienne beams. "And you must tell me where you got that adorable wrap skirt!"

"I made it myself!"

"I can tell that we're going to get along beautifully," she says grandly, sweeping Kelli up and taking her away—probably to look at costume ideas and continue their mutual admiration society.

"I can't believe there are *two* of them," Lauren says. "What have we done?"

I grin. "At least Kelli will be too busy to revive the musical."

"Musical?" Max raises an eyebrow.

"Don't ask," Lauren says.

I'm about to explain, but Daniel literally shoves

himself between me and Max. "Glad you're back, Max! Hey, do you want to see my goose moves?"

Quickly, Tina says, "I think we need to work on those moves a bit more before we show Max." She gently steers him away. "Let's go practice, okay?"

As she leads him away, Daniel says to Max. "Don't go anywhere! I'll be right back!"

Lauren glances at us. "You know, I need to find out what happened to my megaphone. I think Lincoln had it last." She goes off to the side of the stage and starts texting.

That just leaves Max and me.

My neck suddenly feels hot and itchy. "So . . ." I pull at the collar of my shirt. "How did you get your parents to let you come back?"

He shrugs. "They didn't, but I couldn't just leave you all."

He stood up to his parents to help with our dance. I try to be all casual about sniffling into my sleeve. "What about your Chinese school?"

A stubborn glint comes into his eyes. "I'm boycotting it." Then he clears his throat. "Actually, that might be a problem. My parents said they won't build a dance studio unless I go to Chinese school."

Great. The one good thing in the Zhangs' plans was the dance studio. Not only would Max get a place to do something he loves, but Vivienne would have another reason to stay. My stomach turns over at the thought of Vivienne leaving Clarktown and breaking Auntie Li's heart again. But at least Max is here now.

"Thanks for coming back. And for taking the part of the thief."

"Yeah, well . . ." He scuffs his toe on the floor. "I don't think the fundraiser will change anything." He looks up at me. "But I know it's important to you, so I want to help. That's what friends do, right?"

A bubble of happiness rises in me. "Right. And we're friends."

We're looking at each other and grinning when Lauren walks back to us.

"I don't think I can be of much more use here." She's already looking toward the door. "I'm going to head out."

"Petition or picket?" I ask.

"Actually, I think I'll check out the community center," she says, eyes glowing. "You've reminded me of how important it is to our town. I'd forgotten how many classes and clubs are here." *Ah, op-ed, maybe.*

As she talks, I pick up the tablet I had put aside and start recording her.

"Um, is she okay with you doing that?" Max asks.

"Shhh!" I say.

Lauren just smiles and keeps talking directly into my camera. "I guess the community center is a place where anything can happen." Then she turns to Max. "Lily does this all the time. I'm used to it."

With a jolt, I realize how long it's been since I've randomly recorded something. The film had become a stressful thing I was hiding from my friends and family, and somewhere along the line, filming had stopped being fun for me. But this . . . this feels right. Like coming back to myself.

Tina and Daniel come over at that moment. "We have a big problem," Tina announces.

Great. What now?

Tina takes a big breath. "Yesterday, Julia told me that her best friend at school told her that her mother told her—"

"Tina!" I put a hand to my head. "Just tell me, please."

"I think the Knitting League is performing in the showcase too."

"Oh no." My skin goes cold.

Daniel's face scrunches up. "Does Dad know about this? The Quilting Club is going to freak out."

Max looks startled. "I don't get how this is a problem."

"You have no idea," I say grimly. Raising my voice, I call out, "Vivienne, do you know what the other acts are?"

Vivienne walks over with Kelli trailing her. "I think I have the most recent list on my phone." She scrolls through her phone and then drops it into my palm. Without waiting to see what I'm doing, she makes her way to the auditorium doors to welcome in the other kids, who are just starting to come in. Kelli stays to peer curiously over my shoulder with Max and Tina.

I zoom in on the list of acts. I was right about the Chess Club juggling act except that *life-sized* has been crossed out. Now it's just *big* chess pieces. At any other time, I'd crack a joke about literal downsizing, but I'm too busy scrolling through the acts. Star Trek Club. Quilting Club. Zumba. Preschool skit. There it is. *Knitting League.*

I raise my eyes from Vivienne's phone. "This is bad. This is very bad."

Lauren drifts over at that moment, and Kelli asks her, "Do you know what they're talking about?"

"No clue," she replies.

I sigh. "It's the Knitting League and Quilting Club feud. It's been going on forever, but it got worse when the Knitting League did a knit-a-thon that was a rip-off of the quilt-a-thon." Dad tries to stay out of the feud, but even he was annoyed about the knit-a-thon.

"Don't forget about the Crocheting Society taking the Quilting Club's side," Tina reminds me.

"Oh yeah," I say. "No one saw that coming."

Max blinks slowly. "So your point is . . ."

"Right." I wave Vivienne's phone. "My point is that this feud is going to ruin the entire showcase. I've seen them fight, and trust me, if they go at each other during the showcase, they'll make the Chess Club jugglers drop their not-quite-life-sized chess pieces." I can just imagine it. Grown-ups from the Knitting League yelling at grown-ups from the Quilting Club during the preschool skits. "I wouldn't be surprised if the preschoolers end up melting down in the middle of . . ." I squint at the phone. "*Katie the Kindness Koala*?"

"Sounds like a musical." Lauren shudders.

I nod, barely listening. "Lauren, you're right."

"About the preschool musical?"

"No idea," I say. "I mean that you're right that the Clarktown Community Center is important to this town." I pick up my tablet. "And that's why we have to make sure the fundraiser goes perfectly."

Luckily, I know just what to do.

TWENTY-FOUR

THE PRESIDENT OF THE KNITTING League, a representative of the Quilting Club (a.k.a. Dad), and the chair of the Crocheting Society are walking down the narrow hallway of the Clarktown Community Center as if they're going to their execution.

Lauren, Kelli, and I are trailing them and exchanging anxious glances.

"Are we sure this is going to work?" Lauren asks.

"Like I said, if the Knitting League and the Quilting Club keep fighting over their acts, they could ruin the whole fundraiser," I say. "We have to end the feud once and for all."

Kelli shrugs. "It seems bonkers to me, but you know this place the best."

We come to a stop at the multipurpose room, and I hit record on my tablet. If we actually succeed in making peace, I want evidence.

"Here?" Dad asks doubtfully.

"Yup," I say, keeping Dad in the shot as he walks up to the door and knocks.

Stacey, wearing a Starfleet officer cosplay outfit, opens the door for us. I zoom in on her as she says, "Yl'el!"

I'm guessing that means "welcome" in Klingon, and I make a mental note to add subtitles to my video later. "Thanks for agreeing to host this, um, summit."

"The United Federation of Planets is happy to arbitrate intergalactic disputes," she says grandly as two Vulcans, a Klingon, a Borg, and another Starfleet officer rise from their seats behind a long table.

Despite the pointy ears, I recognize one of the Vulcans as Vince, an older kid who left our Chinese school just as I was starting. He must be in college now.

"Right." Lauren blinks at the assembled fan club. "I'm not sure if this qualifies as intergalactic. Everyone's from the same . . . planet."

I wish Max were here to see this. It's just the kind of weird and wonderful he would love. Unfortunately, he couldn't get away from his family; it's all he can do to sneak away for the dance rehearsals.

"We're actually a neutral party and not a part of this dispute," Ms. Green, the president of the Crocheting Society pipes up.

Ms. Taylor, the president of the Knitting League,

snorts. "Last time I checked, *neutral* didn't mean a joint booth with the Quilting Club at the Clarktown Summer Festival."

Dad looks panicked and is slowly backing away, toward the door. He hates conflict and only agreed to come because I begged him to.

I pin Dad with a warning look. We'd better begin before the Quilting Club representative bolts. "Stacey . . . I mean, Captain, don't you think it's time to get started?"

"It's 'Admiral,' actually," she says, but she sits down behind the long table and says commandingly, "All parties, please approach the Federation."

Lauren comes with me to talk to the Fencing Team, not that I think I'll need any help with this next mission. To her credit, she doesn't immediately make a beeline for Glenn even though they visibly perk up and look at Lauren like she's just made their day. Nice to see that Glenn is well on their way to smittenville . . . although I would expect nothing less. You'd have to be dead inside not to realize how amazing my best friend is.

"Sorry to interrupt," I say as the Fencing Team turns away from the duel in progress to stare curiously at us. "I'm here to ask if you would all like to be extras in the Chinese school dance performance for the fundraiser showcase."

One of the masked duelists lowers his sword . . . foil,

I correct myself. Judging from the thinner blade and smaller guard of the sword, it's a foil (see, I was totally paying attention to the lecture on the different fencing swords I got the last time I was here). The duelist takes off his helmet, and it's Adam, the teenager who used to go to our Chinese school. "Are you kidding?" he says excitedly. "That would be awesome!"

The others all agree, and then Glenn looks at Lauren. "You should totally perform with us! You're getting really good!"

What? My eyebrows rise. "Since when do you fence?" I whisper to her.

"You're not the only one with a double life," Lauren whispers back to me before replying to Glenn, "I would love to."

Taking pity on me as I continue to stare at her with my mouth hanging open, she adds, "Glenn has been teaching me ever since we connected on that first day of filming." She blushes. "It's fun, actually."

I'm not sure if she means hanging out with Glenn or fencing, but knowing Lauren, it's both. She's not the type to take up an activity just because she has a crush on someone. "It looks like you're going to be an extra as a swordswoman in *The Phoenix and Her Community Center*." Then a thought occurs to me. "What is Kelli going to say?"

"Kelli is too busy with costuming the entire cast and all these extras you've recruited to worry about whether or not she has a part in the dance performance," Lauren says calmly.

She has a point. At this very moment, Kelli is talking to the Creative Anachronism Society about costumes. She'll probably be ecstatic about dressing up the entire Fencing Team.

Reminded, I turn back to Adam. "I'm thinking of you all sword fighting in the background of the dance to hint at epic battles in the mortal world while the fan dancers as the phoenixes dance on their mountaintop," I say. "Are you up for choreographing it?"

"Oh yeah," he breathes, closing his eyes as if he can visualize it already. Then his eyes pop back open. "Wait. Did you say mountaintop? How's that going to work?"

I grin at him. "Leave that up to me."

Next stop, the Art Club.

"So you're sure it's not too much?" I ask Joanne. "I mean, it will mean a few different backdrops—the mountain-top, the dying town, and the town that's come back to life."

"It won't be a problem." Joanne puts her long black hair into a ponytail. "The community center is our home too."

The other Art Club kids, a mix of high school teens, middle schoolers, and a few older elementary school kids, all chime in.

"That's right!"

"Yeah."

"Besides," Joanne says, "I don't want to lose the school." She means Hong Chinese Academy, where she used to go.

I stare at Joanne's determined face. Vince, Adam, Joanne—they all want to help save their former Chinese school. A startling realization is starting to form. I'd thought that all the Chinese kids leave our school because they never wanted to be there, but what if I was wrong? After all, the school is still under their feet in the basement of the community center that is home to their Star Trek Fan Club, Fencing Team, and Art Club.

Maybe they haven't really left us.

TWENTY-FIVE

AFTER DANCE PRACTICE, LAUREN AND I pick up Kelli from the preschool (she's helping with their costumes too). It turns out that *Katie the Kindness Koala* actually *is* a musical. Ms. Leticia and the preschoolers don't know how lucky they are that Kelli limited herself to helping with costumes instead of taking over their musical. They're also lucky that the Creative Anachronism Society didn't have their way in making a medieval koala costume.

Kelli is writing down something when we enter the preschool, but she tosses the notebook into her backpack along with her measuring tape and hurries to join us. "Let's go," she whispers, "while we still can."

Ms. Leticia is talking to a preschooler in braids when we enter her classroom. "Cindi," Ms. Leticia says, "that's a, um, lovely program." She holds up a sheet of paper dripping with glue and glitter. "But it might have a little too much glitter glue. Let's try it again. Ms. Moreno will be here soon with more programs to decorate." The preschoolers have been given the task of decorating the covers of the showcase programs. Which means that each one will be . . . unique.

"I like it." Cindi's mouth sets into a pout as she grabs the glittery program. She's the kid who plays Katie the Kindness Koala, and her eyes turn to Kelli, Lauren, and me. "What do *they* think?" she demands, pointing at us.

I like any kid who's willing to die on the hill for glitter, but I'm not about to get in the middle of this. "Sorry—" I start to say, but she plants herself right in front of me.

"Are you the girl who saw the Knitting League ghost?" she demands. The glittery program falls from her hand, apparently forgotten.

"Uh, I didn't actually see her, but I did hear her one time in the basement where the Chinese school is."

"*Did you?*" Kelli asks, drawing out the words to emphasize her skepticism.

Lauren glances at her watch. "We promised Tina and Max we'd meet them for ice cream as soon as we got Kelli."

I nod. "Good luck finding the Knitting League ghost," I say, scooting around Cindi to make my escape with Kelli and Lauren.

We almost bump into Ms. Moreno, who's walking toward the preschool with an armful of programs.

"Girls," she says, "have you seen the programs yet?" She hands us each a program with a blank white cover.

I open up the program, and our dance jumps out at me. It's listed last in a larger font than the other acts. And that's not all.

Headliner
The Phoenix and Her Community Center:
A Chinese Classical Dance
Performed by Hong Chinese Academy Dancers
Choreographed by Vivienne Hou
Original Script by Lily Hong

My jaw drops. "But . . . but . . ." I sputter. "How is there a headliner? Won't the other acts be mad?"

"Everyone agreed," Ms. Moreno says. "We all know your dance performance will be the biggest draw, so why not make sure it has top billing?"

"That's awesome!" Kelli says excitedly.

"It really is the best script you've ever done," Lauren says. "Better than *The Tragic Romance of Medusa*, even."

My heart is flooded with emotion as I stare down at my name on the clean white pages of the program . . . unless Cindi and her glitter glue get to it. "Can I keep this one?"

"Of course." Ms. Moreno's eyes turn misty. "You might as well have something to remember this place."

"Don't say that, Ms. Moreno. The fundraiser will make enough to save the center." *But just in case . . .* I put the program in my backpack and take out my tablet. "Could you talk a little about the community center, Ms. Moreno?"

"Me?" She laughs nervously and runs a hand through her hair. "I suppose I could. Let's see, what do I say?"

"Just talk about what it means to you." I focus on Ms. Moreno and start recording.

"I can do that." The nervousness melts off her face. "This might have been my dream, but so many people have found and followed their own dreams here. The center is more than a place." She smiles at me. "It's where we build community and friendships."

It certainly is. A lump forms in my throat as Lauren and Kelli move closer to me.

"Was that okay?" Ms. Moreno asks.

I stop the recording. "It was perfect."

Ms. Moreno peers into the preschool classroom. "I'd better get these other programs to Leticia and the kids. I can't believe the showcase is tomorrow!"

Lauren, Kelli, and I exchange anxious glances.

Can we really pull this off and save the community center?

The lobby of the auditorium is filled with quilts and knitted and crocheted crafts. As part of the truce negotiated by the United Federation of Planets, all three craft clubs have dropped out of the showcase and are contributing to the fundraiser by selling crafts before the show and during the intermission.

Dad is sitting in front of a table with a quilt representing the Federation planets (the Star Trek Fan Club included that as a clause in the treaty) hanging on the wall behind him.

Daniel is helping Dad sell quilts, Mom is at the ticket booth with Ms. Moreno, Kelli is with her dad, selling frozen treats at the concession stand, Lauren is warming up with the Fencing Team, and Tina and I are looking at knitted and crocheted hats (honestly, I can't tell the difference despite both groups insisting they're completely different).

I'm considering a hat with the Star Trek logo when Ms. Leticia bursts into the lobby, followed by what looks like most of the Fencing Team (including Lauren) in white outfits with colorful sashes, several knights and ladies who must be from the Creative Anachronism Society, and a few others. Ms. Leticia's normally neat hair is escaping its ponytail, and she's panting and wild-eyed. "Two preschoolers are missing!"

Oh no. My fingers turn numb, and I drop the hat I was holding. Everyone else in the lobby also falls silent and turns to Ms. Leticia.

Relax. This is Clarktown. I'm sure the kids will be fine,

but when Tina clutches my hand, I squeeze back hard.

My mother leaves the ticket booth immediately and goes to Ms. Leticia. "Which ones?" Her voice is tense.

"Cindi and Hana." Ms. Leticia takes a breath. "They're both in the preschool act, but when I went backstage just now, they were gone. I can't find them anywhere."

"We scoured ye olde auditorium—" a knight begins, but a woman in a long green gown and matching head-dress interrupts him.

"Not now, Sir Kyle," she says.

Cindi, the kid with the glitter programs is missing— the one who was so interested in the Knitting League ghost. My heart starts racing. "I think I know where they are."

Trekkies, the Fencing Team (at least they left their épées, foils, and sabers backstage), and everyone else, including Tina, Lauren, Kelli, my parents, and me, race down the hallway of the community center. Everyone wants to be a part of the rescue mission, but we make so much noise clattering down the steps to the basement that Cindi and Hana will probably think the Knitting League ghost is coming for them.

Sure enough, when we burst into the Chinese school classroom, a small koala and an even smaller elephant are huddled under one of the desks, staring at us with wide eyes.

Ms. Leticia rushes over to them. "Cindi! Hana! What are you doing here?"

"We wanted to see the Knitting League ghost," Cindi says.

Hana scans the room from under the desk. "Yeah! Is she here?" Neither girl looks like she's going to budge.

"There's no such thing as a Knitting League ghost," Ms. Taylor says scornfully. "Ghosts don't exist." *Doesn't she know that will just make them more determined to prove the existence of the ghost?*

Cindi's chin lifts. "They do too."

"I'm not leaving until I see her," Hana says.

Ms. Leticia squats down in front of the desk. "Why do you think there's a ghost here?"

Uh-oh. My skin turns hot and sweaty.

Cindi points right at me and says, "*She* said there was!" Of course she ratted me out. *What did I expect from a four-year-old?*

"I . . . uh," I sputter as all eyes turn to me.

Ms. Leticia stands up and looks at me, but she doesn't seem angry. "Lily, can you come here and talk to the girls?" She steps away from the desk. "The show starts in half an hour, and the preschool is the first act. It's not going to be good if the stars of our musical are no-shows because they're in the basement ghost hunting."

Right. But what can I do? "Um, I guess I can try." On numb legs, I walk over and squat in front of the two kids.

"Hey," I say, totally winging it. "So, uh, the Knitting League ghost is real, but grown-ups can't see her."

"Why not?" Cindi and Hana ask at the same time.

Okay, fair question, and one that I don't have an answer to. "I'll tell you the story of . . . Nettie the Knitting League Ghost later, but right now, Nettie needs your help."

"Our help?" Hana asks.

"Yeah." I touch the trunk coming out of her mask and one of Cindi's furry ears. I'm starting to warm up to my story. "Nettie needs the Kindness Koala and the Empathy Elephant to put on the best performance ever so we can save her home."

Cindi and Hana look at each other and crawl out from under the desk. A relieved Ms. Leticia gathers them up, and everyone starts cheering.

"You know you'll have to come up with a Nettie the Knitting League Ghost story now," Lauren comments when she, Kelli, and Tina make their way to me.

"Not a problem." Nettie's story is already starting to take shape in my imagination.

"Nettie the Knitting League Ghost?" Kelli asks with a snicker.

"I take my inspiration from the environment," I say with as much dignity as I can muster, "and I was talking to Katie the Kindness Koala and Ellie the Empathy Elephant."

"Fair enough." Then, in a rapid change of subject, she

asks, "Hey, will you need costumes for the story?" Knowing Kelli, she's thinking of fake blood and decomposing flesh—definitely not preschooler-friendly.

"Um, let's keep it simple this time," I say.

"Nice job of getting the kids out from under that desk." Tina pats my back. "Didn't you tell us a Knitting League ghost story at Chinese school camp that one time?"

"Yeah," I say sheepishly. "I think that's why we ended up barricading ourselves in. We're lucky Cindi and Hana didn't think of that." I glance at everyone else trooping out of the classroom. "Let's get back upstairs. The show's about to start."

"Remember that the tripod is your friend," I tell Dad anxiously. "Don't try to be a hero and take the tablet off the tripod. I have it set up at the best angle to get the whole stage."

"I have done video recordings before," he says dryly. "And don't you need to get ready for your performance?"

I smooth down my embroidered sash and pat my hair, which is secured by so many bobby pins and so much hair spray that it would take a hurricane to move it out of place. "I'm already dressed."

He squints up at the stage. "I think Vivienne is waving at you to get backstage."

I sigh, looking around the theater. *There are a lot of empty seats.* "We have time. The showcase won't start for another fifteen minutes, and the theater isn't even half full yet!"

"More people will come. Just focus on the dance you worked so hard on." He opens up a program with a rainbow drawn in crayon on the cover. "Look at that!" he says. "'Original script by Lily Hong.' My daughter is a writer!"

"Filmmaker," I correct him. Worry churns in my stomach as I peer at the preschoolers, who are racing each other down the aisles. They're supposed to be handing out programs, but there's no one else coming in. "I think I'll go check on Mom." She's at the ticket booth with Ms. Moreno and Lauren's parents, and she can tell me how much money the show has made so far.

Gently, Dad steers me toward the door to the backstage. "There's nothing more you can do."

The muscles in my neck tense up, but Dad is right. "Leave the tablet on the tripod," I say again, "and make sure to get all the performances. Not just ours."

"I've got this, Lily. Go have fun!"

How can I have fun when the community center is in danger? But my spirits lift as I walk backstage. The Chess Club is practicing their juggling, the senior citizens are warming up for the Zumba demonstration, a Klingon is bellowing his lines, Lauren and the Fencing Team are practicing the choreography for our performance, and Tina, Daniel, and the others are flicking their fans expertly under Vivienne's guidance. Auntie Li is handing out water and snacks, and Kelli is helping everyone with hair and makeup. I ache for my tablet to document all this.

"Hey, do you want to borrow this?" Max, wearing silk black pants and a matching embroidered vest, is holding a sleek silver camcorder out to me.

"Seriously?" But I'm already taking the camcorder and zooming in on the Chess Club juggling. "Thanks!"

He smiles. "No problem. I figured you'd be getting antsy without your camera."

I look up from the camcorder screen, warmth spreading through my chest. He might still not understand why the community center is so important to all of us, but no one can say he isn't being a hundred percent supportive.

"Lily," Vivienne calls out. "Are you ready?"

A week ago, she would have just patted me on the shoulder and said, "Try your best." But this past week, whenever I haven't been filming, sleeping, eating, or doing schoolwork, I've had a fan in my hand.

"Totally." I hand Max the camcorder and pick up two fans. With a flick of my wrists, the fans open into perfect arches of red, green, gold, black, and white—the phoenix's colors, which the Art Club painted onto our fans. I flutter one in front and one behind me like a tail, and then I bring one to my waist and flip the other one into the air—catching it on the way down with one hand.

There are actually tears in Vivienne's eyes. "You're ready," she says.

TWENTY-SIX

THE AUDIENCE GASPS AUDIBLY AS Max plunges a plastic dagger into a piece of Astroturf where we've hidden a packet of fake blood (repurposed from *The Chosen One Slays Big Business on the Hellmouth*). The stage runs with rivulets of red, and Max does a triumphant leap into the air, holding up a heart the Art Club made from modeling clay. "At last! I have the heart of the phoenix. I will bring it to my own town, and it will prosper!"

Tina cries out, "Someone has stolen my heart that I transformed into the town's community center! What will happen to my beloved town without its heart?" Her red, yellow, green, black, and white sashes flutter behind her as she falls to the ground and snaps her multicolored fans closed.

The audience gasps again.

Daniel, as the goose in all white, flutters over to us, the

phoenix sisters. "A thief has stolen your younger sister's heart! The villagers have lost their community center! What will we do?"

"Kill the thief!" Julia yells, lifting her fan like a weapon. "Avenge our sister!"

That's my cue. My skin goes damp because this is the first of my few speaking parts in the performance, and I do *not* want to mess it up like I did in *The Wizard of Clarktown* (and *The Chosen One Slays Big Business on the Hellmouth: A Musical in Three Parts*). But these are the lines I wrote myself—and I believe in them. Taking a deep breath, I step forward. "No. The thief doesn't know what he has done. We must help him understand."

"Very well, sister," Julia says, and I don't know if she's acting or if she really wanted to use her fan as a weapon, but the reluctance in her voice is perfect. "But if he won't listen, then we attack!"

Julia leads us to Max, and we circle him, lifting and lowering our fans to form a wave that alternately hides him and reveals him to the audience.

Max quickly stuffs the clay heart into the pouch at his waist. "Who are you?" he asks, twisting and leaping like he's trying to escape the cage of wings we've formed around him. "What do you want with me?" Then he brandishes his plastic dagger and lunges at us.

The others peel off, flapping their wings furiously, but I stay and face Max alone.

We stare at each other and wait tensely for our cue.

It comes with a thunder of cymbals through the speakers, and someone in the audience shrieks as Max and I launch ourselves at each other. But I'm too busy with the steps of our choreographed dance fight to spare a glance at the audience.

My closed fan meets his dagger, and I spin away, snapping open my fan and attacking again, knocking the dagger out of his hands with my multicolored feathers. He somersaults under the swoop of feathers I aim just above his head and recovers his dagger. Then we parry and dodge again.

At last, Max drops the dagger and crouches with his head hanging as if he's exhausted by our fight. Pretending not to notice him, I slowly back up until I feel his hands grip me under my arms. With his help, I climb onto the platform of his thighs, and his hands anchor me in place.

Peering side to side, I cry out, "Where is he?"

A kid in the audience calls out, "He's right behind you!"

"That's my line!" Daniel yells indignantly, and the audience laughs.

This throws me off, and for a panicked moment, I can't remember what comes next. Max's thighs quiver, making me struggle to stay balanced. He can't support me much longer. . . . *Oh! I remember.* "Thief!" I shout. "I've found you!"

That's Max's cue to pretend to push me away. I leap off him, and then we leap at each other, my open fan at his throat, and his dagger at the side of my neck. The plastic feels cool against my heated skin, and we're both panting from exertion.

"It looks like we're evenly matched, phoenix," he says.

"You're right, thief. Neither of us will win this way." I pull my fan back from his throat and snap it shut. "Let's call a truce."

Max's eyes glint as if he's remembering the real truce we called nearly a month ago. "Agreed. Truce." He drops the dagger. "But why did you and the other phoenixes attack me?"

"You have stolen our little sister's heart!" I say. "She turned her body into protection for this village, and without the community center as the heart, this village will die."

"I didn't know." He's supposed to act shocked and horrified as he looks toward Tina, collapsed on the floor among her colorful sashes, but instead, he's locking gazes with me. His voice is low and serious. "I'm sorry."

A lump forms in my throat. "What will you do now?"

He takes the clay heart out of his pouch and holds it out to me with a graceful flourish. "Take back the heart of your village."

My fingers brush his as I take it, and my own chest flutters as if something has just been returned to my body.

Tina spreads open her multicolored fans. She is glorious as she rises, trailing sashes like plumage and waving her fans like the wings of the phoenix. "My heart has been returned and the town's community center is saved!"

The audience bursts into applause, and we all line up to take a bow.

Then I look out at the dusty theater and see row after row of empty seats, and my gut wrenches.

There's no way we raised enough money to save the center.

After the show, Lauren, Kelli, and Tina watch from my bed as I go through the footage of the show. Mom is letting me use her laptop, and I've already transferred the footage from my tablet and the video camera I borrowed from Max.

"It's too bad all that work for the fundraiser was for nothing," Kelli says glumly.

Lauren sighs. "Yeah." It's bad when she isn't even planning a rally.

"I can't believe it's over." Tina's eyes glisten with tears.

I pause on Ms. Moreno welcoming the audience. Then I spin around in my seat to face my friends. "Are we really going to give up?"

Kelli throws up her hands. "What can we do?"

"Lily, we raised only five thousand dollars from the talent show, including the concessions and crafts sold,"

Lauren says. "That leaves us ninety-five thousand dollars short of the down payment the nonprofit needs to buy the center."

Tina bites her lip. "That's a lot of money."

"I know." I turn back to the laptop. Hopelessness overtakes me when I look at Ms. Moreno's face, frozen on my screen. She had been worried that the fundraiser wouldn't be enough. "I'm going to put together a video about the center for Ms. Moreno. It will help her remember it."

The three of them talk as I start editing, and I block them out as I put together the story of our community center. Ms. Leticia herding the preschoolers as they pass out hand-decorated programs. Ms. Moreno talking about her family's history with the center. Clips from the Fencing Team, the Art Club, and the Star Trek arbitration meeting. Footage I had of the Chinese school kids barricading the doors against the Knitting League ghost and Lauren's parents leading a community meeting about immigrant rights. Even a clip from our film, shot in that long hallway in the community center with Lauren saying in voice-over, "I guess the community center is a place where anything can happen." Many more scenes. Throughout the film, I splice in pieces from our dance performance to create a clear narrative.

I finish editing just as Mom knocks on the door. "It's almost curfew," she says. "I'll drive your friends home."

"Can we have ten more minutes?" I ask. "I just finished a video about the community center and want to show it to them."

"Of course." She opens the door and walks in. "I'd like to see it too if that's okay."

I nod, a little surprised.

My mom clears a pile of clothes off my chair before sitting down, and my friends scoot over on the bed to make a space for me.

I hit play on the laptop, and we watch the video together.

Fifteen minutes later, the video ends with Tina rising from the floor of the stage as the phoenix reborn.

The credits roll, and it's dead silent. My stomach lurches. Why isn't anyone saying anything? Was it that bad?

The quiet is broken by a sniffle. Mom wipes her eyes. "Lily, it's beautiful. I had no idea you could make something so . . . moving."

Tears stream down Kelli's face. "It really is amazing."

"You showed how important the center is." Lauren sounds choked up. "Ms. Moreno is going to love it."

Tina hugs me. "Good job, Lily."

Hot wetness stings my own eyes. How can we let the center go? It really *is* the heart of Clarktown. We might not die without it, but like Ms. Moreno said, we'll lose more than just a place. We'll lose something of ourselves.

When my mom and my friends leave, I go to the laptop and send the video to Ms. Moreno, but I hesitate before turning the laptop off.

There's one more thing I need to do. Max helped us out because he felt bad about me losing the center, but I don't know if I was ever really able to show him how important it is to the whole town. Maybe my video can show him that.

I send Max my video too.

TWENTY-SEVEN

—

ON MONDAY MORNING, ALL EYES turn to Lauren, Kelli, and me as we walk into seventh-grade Honors English. Max and Mr. Orwell are huddled over the computer at the front of the class, but they look up as we enter the room. *What's going on?*

I haven't seen Max since the talent show on Friday, but this is not how I imagined our meeting. I thought he would be all awkward and regretful—not practically bursting with excitement. Did he even watch my film? He sent me a text over the weekend to say he got it, but there was nothing but radio silence after that.

"Lily!" he calls out. "Wait until you see this!"

"Let's show them!" Mr. Orwell grins before looking back at the monitor. "You've really done something special here, Max."

You've got to be kidding me. It's bad enough that Mr.

Orwell is making such a big deal about *Of Mice and Mazes* finally getting uploaded to the school website, but what really makes me angry is that Max seems to have forgotten all about the community center.

Rage burning in my heart, I take a step toward Max.

Alarm flashes across his face, and he takes a step backward. But then, unbelievably—he has the gall to smile at me.

Oh, Max Zhang is going *down*.

On either side of me, Lauren and Kelli take hold of my arms, and without a word, they steer me to my desk.

"Calm down," Lauren says, pushing me into my seat.

"You don't want to get suspended for trying to beat up Max," Kelli says.

"I won't be trying to beat him up," I seethe. "I *will* beat him up."

"Then your parents will ground you, and you'll miss our *Buffy* viewing this weekend," Kelli points out. "Remember, we're going to watch the musical episode 'Once More, with Feeling' in season six as inspiration for our film?" Since she was such a good sport about the talent show, I promised her a script rewrite of *The Chosen One Slays Big Business on the Hellmouth* as a musical.

My friends sit on either side of me as I huff my breath out in short, furious bursts. "I can't believe we have to watch *Of Mice and Mazes* right now!"

Mr. Orwell dims the lights, and Max shoots me an

unreadable look before sitting down at his own desk.

Resentfully, I wait for Max's voice to come over the speakers and the opening image of the rat racing through a maze to be projected onto the screen.

But the dark, claustrophobic shot of the maze never appears. Instead, the shot is light-filled. The opening image of the Clarktown Community Center comes onto the screen.

"Oh wow," Lauren whispers next to me as Ms. Moreno's voice comes out of the speakers in a voice-over. *This might have been my dream, but so many people have found and followed their own dreams here. The center is more than a place. It's where we build community and friendships.*

It's not Max's film. It's mine.

Shock floods me. Is Max trying to pass off my film as his own? But no—my name is right there in the opening credits.

I'm so stunned that I'm frozen in place for a full five minutes—until the scene with Max giving me the phoenix's heart back comes on the screen. Dad couldn't resist taking the camera off the tripod to shoot it, but I have to admit the close-up on Max's earnest face and my passionate gestures turned out well. . . .

What am I doing—admiring the camerawork when I should be finding out what the heck is going on?!

Leaping out of my chair, I shriek, "What is happening? Why are we watching my video in class?"

Mr. Orwell hits pause on the remote control and laughs. "Max, do you want to explain why we're showing Lily's excellent film?" He exits full screen, and my eye is drawn to the web address bar at the top of the window.

A Kickstarter campaign site? My mind whirls in confusion.

Max turns around in his seat. "Your film is brilliant, Lily! I knew that if other people saw it, they'd want to help save the community center, so I started a Kickstarter campaign and uploaded your film." His face is all lit up with enthusiasm. "And it worked! Your video has gone viral, and people from all around the world are donating money!"

"Money?" I ask faintly. I can't seem to take in what Max is telling me.

Mr. Orwell clicks a tab on the computer and opens a page that is tracking the donations. My jaw drops in shock. In just two short days, Max's campaign has raised nearly fifty thousand dollars for the Clarktown Community Nonprofit to buy the center.

"Does this mean that we just need fifty thousand more dollars to save the center?" Kelli asks.

"Forty-five thousand, actually, if you include the five thousand that the talent show made." Lauren is grinning from ear to ear.

"You did this?" I ask Max. A warm feeling washes over my body.

"Not really. It's your film that shows people how important the Clarktown Community Center is." Then his face falls. "Besides, it isn't enough yet."

"More donations could come in." For the first time since the talent show, I feel a faint stirring of hope.

Other kids start talking, and Mr. Orwell doesn't even try to call the class to order.

"I'll donate my allowance money!"

"My parents will donate money for sure. They take yoga classes at the center."

"Cool film, Lily!"

Then Kelli screams, "Look!" She's pointing at the Kickstarter campaign on the screen.

An anonymous donor has just given fifty thousand dollars.

Lauren stands up and clutches my hand as I stare at the screen in disbelief, tears running down my face.

The Clarktown Community Center has just been saved.

TWENTY-EIGHT

AS SOON AS SCHOOL IS over, Lauren, Kelli, Max, and I race out the front doors.

"I've got to tell my mom!" Lauren calls over her shoulder as she heads to her mother's law office.

"My parents probably already know, but I'd better make sure," Kelli says as she rushes away.

That just leaves Max and me.

I swallow nervously. "Thanks for using my film to create the Kickstarter campaign."

"I didn't really do anything. It was your film that inspired people to donate."

"You were the one who believed in my film. I never would have thought it would go viral!"

"You know what?" he says with a smirk. "You're right. I single-handedly saved the center."

"I wouldn't go that far!" I scowl at him.

"Fine!" He holds up his hands. "Why don't we just say we make a good team?"

"Works for me." I grin. "Let's go tell everyone the good news. Race you there!" Without warning, I take off at a dead run for the community center.

"Hey! You got a head start. You're cheating!"

But he catches up right as we reach the center, and we burst through the front doors together.

Panting, we come to a halt in the entryway. Then my pounding heart sinks.

Ms. Zhang is standing with Mom and Vivienne at the front desk, and they all turn toward us. The door behind the desk is open, and I catch a glimpse of Ms. Moreno and Ms. Leticia whispering to each other in the back office.

Is Max's mom still trying to buy the center? There's no way the Morenos will sell to the Zhangs if they can sell it to the nonprofit instead, but this is bad news for Max. Especially if they find out that Max is the one who started the Kickstarter campaign that caused his parents to lose out on getting the center.

Max and I glance at each other and then walk up to the front desk together.

"Mom," he says stiffly, "what are you doing here?"

"Well, I had to come by to pay Principal Hong for the dance lessons you secretly took from Ms. Hou."

He hunches his shoulders. "Right."

Vivienne waves an airy hand. "It was a pleasure to teach such a talented student!" Her eyes fall on me. "*All* my students are a delight, of course!"

To my utter shock, Ms. Zhang smiles at me. "I'm sure they are. But that doesn't mean you should teach for free." She hands a check to Mom. "Here you go, Sara. That should cover Max's previous lessons as well as lessons for the rest of the school year."

Does that mean what I think it means?

Max sucks his breath in sharply. "So I can take dance classes with Vivienne?"

"I certainly hope so," she says, "or else I've just paid for nothing."

He releases his breath in an audible whoosh.

Mom holds the check as if she's not sure what to do with it. "As I explained, Ms. Zhang, there's no need to pay that far in advance."

"Call me Elizabeth," Ms. Zhang says.

"Of course," Mom says without calling her anything at all. Then she looks uncertainly at Vivienne. "The thing is—I'm not entirely sure how long our dance teacher is planning to stay."

"Oh, I'm here to stay." There's an unusual firmness to Vivienne's voice. "There's nowhere I'd rather be."

Joy springs up in me. Auntie Li will be happy, and Max gets dance lessons.

"But, Mom," Max says, "I thought you said I couldn't

take dance classes after school! What changed your mind?"

I nudge him sharply in the ribs. *Stop asking questions and just accept this miracle.*

"I saw your dancing, Max," his mom says softly. "You were wonderful in that performance. I never knew you were so talented."

Max flushes, but he's smiling.

"I know what you mean," Mom says. "Sometimes we miss what our children are capable of."

The pride in her voice unfurls something in my chest. I'm glad I showed her my film.

Then Ms. Zhang's words echo in my mind. She wasn't at the talent show, so how did she see Max dance? I look at her. "Did you see the film?"

"If you mean your film that my son uploaded to a Kickstarter campaign, then yes—I did."

"Oh." My throat goes dry, but amazingly, she's still smiling.

"It was a lovely film, Lily," she says. "In fact, I was inspired to donate myself."

Realization hits me like a thunderclap. "It was *you*! You donated the fifty thousand to get us to our goal of buying the center!"

Her cheeks turn pink. "Like I said, it was a good film."

"What's this?" my mother asks, a puzzled expression in her eyes.

I whip out my tablet and show Mom the Kickstarter campaign.

She turns to Ms. Zhang with a look of awe on her face. "I can't believe you did this." Then she looks at Max and me. "What you all did—it's amazing."

Vivienne peers over her shoulder at my tablet. "How wonderful!"

"I wanted to do something for our new home." Ms. Zhang plucks at the strap of her designer purse. "I guess a high-rise wasn't what this town needs. It needs this community center. Your film showed me that, Lily." She wraps her arms around Max. "And it also showed me what my son loves. Thank you."

I know she's talking about Max's love of dance and not . . . anything else, but my face flares up anyway. "You're welcome," I mumble.

Ms. Moreno and Ms. Leticia come out of the back office. "We just saw the Kickstarter campaign video that Lily made," Ms. Leticia says excitedly. "Now we can sell the center to the Clarktown Community Nonprofit!"

Ms. Moreno sweeps me up in a big hug. "It was a beautiful video, Lily. Thank you. For everything."

My cheeks warm, and I don't know what to say. "No problem."

Ms. Moreno's face is still glowing as she releases me and turns to my mother. "Sara, we've all discussed it and have come to an agreement. Leticia and I will be happy to be on the board of the nonprofit, and Janet will also be on the board to provide legal counsel, but we agree that *you* should be the center's director!"

"Me?" Mom looks stunned.

"Definitely," Ms. Leticia says. "I have my hands full managing the preschool. You've been practically running the center anyway. This just makes it official."

Mom's expression becomes thoughtful. "I'll think about it." She glances at me. "And I need to talk to my family, of course."

That means my mother is the new Clarktown Community Center director because I already know what we'll all say. "You should definitely do it, Mom!" I'm so proud of her that I could scream, but I settle for giving her a big hug.

"Thank you, Lily." She hugs me back.

Max turns to his mother. "So, just to be clear . . . I can take dance classes with Vivienne after school and not go to Chinese school anymore?"

"Oh no," she says. "You still need to go to Chinese school, but maybe not in Seattle. Luckily, there's an excellent Saturday Chinese school right here in Clark-town."

Mom blinks, and then a smile spreads over her face. Not her fake one—her real smile. "We would love to have Max at our school." She pauses and adds, "By the way, some of us have been doing a book club for many years now. I don't suppose you'd like to join us, Elizabeth?" *Did she just call Ms. Zhang by her first name?*

Ms. Zhang's whole face lights up. "I would love to!" She looks like she just won the lottery.

I poke Max in the arm. "I guess this means I'm going to have to step up my Chinese school game to beat you." Auntie Li is going to be shocked when I come to school on Saturday with my homework as perfect as I can get it, and without my baggie of pennies.

Max grins. "You don't have to compete with me." Then his voice turns serious. "You're one of a kind, Lily Hong. Unbeatable."

TWENTY-NINE
—

"WHO'S UP FOR BONUS OUTTAKES?" I ask as we eat ice cream at Ice Yum Palace.

Kelli's dad always lets us eat for free, but this time, he outdid himself. To celebrate the saving of the community center, he's made us the biggest banana fudge sundae I've ever seen. Twelve scoops, all different flavors, four whole bananas, a gallon of fudge, heaps of whipped cream, and about a million maraschino cherries.

"You'd better not be kidding," Max says, clutching his heart and looking at my other friends. "Please tell me she actually has outtakes and isn't just messing with us."

"I'm sure she does," Lauren says calmly, scooping up some of the strawberry ice cream.

"I'd love to see that, Lily," Tina says, eyeing the sundae like she's not sure it's real.

I'm so glad that Tina is a part of this friend group now. Max too.

Tina finally digs into the sundae. "Oh, yum."

"Yup, that's why my dad named it Ice Yum Palace." Kelli dabs at a bit of fudge on her mouth. "Okay, I'm ready for outtakes. Let's see it, Lily!"

I grin and set up my tablet on a portable stand. "Here we go, then." I press play.

The preschoolers fill the screen, sitting in a circle as they watch me, gesturing wildly with my hands. "And then Nettie the Knitting League Ghost swore she would leave knitted presents all around the center. . . ."

The scene changes to the entryway of the preschool, where the kids are dropping off their backpacks and coats. A sudden scream of joy pierces the room, and Cindi reaches into her cubbyhole to pull out a little knitted koala.

"I have one too!" Hana shrieks, holding up her elephant.

All the preschoolers start yelling and losing their minds. "It's Nettie the Knitting League Ghost!"

Despite Ms. Taylor's initial protests about supporting such nonsense, the rest of the Knitting League was thrilled to play along, and Ms. Taylor ended up relenting. Now she's acting as if it's her idea, which is fine by me as long as the knitted animals keep coming. The only problem is that Ms. Green cornered me the other day and asked me what I thought of telling a story about Christelle the Crocheting Ghost.

The scene changes again to a practice battle between the Fencing Team and a Klingon wielding his bat'leth and screaming "Heghlu'meH QaQ jajvam." Stacey was kind enough to give me a translation for the subtitles: *Today is a good day to die.* The battle wasn't part of an act or anything—it's just what happens when the Star Trek Club and the Fencing Team are rehearsing at the same time. Lauren leaps forward and thrusts her practice foil at the Klingon like she's been fencing for years.

Then there's a clip with Kelli holding a half-finished koala costume as members of the Creative Anachronism Society call out suggestions.

"How about some chain mail armor?"

"Yeah! With a helmet and a visor."

"Maybe a Renaissance gown?"

"This isn't medieval Build-a-Bear," Kelli says, pulling the costume close to her chest. "This is a koala costume for a preschool skit."

The next outtake is of Ms. Taylor from the Knitting League hugging Dad, who looks extremely uncomfortable. Without letting go of him, she says, "I am so glad we've come to an agreement with the Quilting Club!"

Stacey translates this for the single Klingon in the United Federation of Planets (no one has seen him break character), and he makes a toast, which Stacey translates literally as "May your blood scream," but apparently that's just Klingon for "Cheers." The two Vulcans respond with their usual "Live long and prosper" while doing the Vulcan hand thing.

The next one is blurry because I shot it from behind a bush on the edge of the elementary school playfield, and it's not *technically* an outtake from the community center video, but just call it curiosity on my part.

A teacher is recording some elementary school kids as they play a basketball game. At first, I thought there was no way this video would win the Clarktown's Got Talent contest, but then Louis, the kid who quit our dance, started doing these Globetrotter moves, and the other kids on his team did them too, and it became clear the whole game is choreographed.

On the screen, a kid on the other team bumps into her teammate, and they start falling down like dominoes. . . .

"Hey," Tina says, "that's just what happened to us on the first day of dance rehearsal!" Again, she's too nice to point out that I had caused that disaster.

Without taking my eyes off the screen, I say, "I can't prove it, but I think Louis stole our routine . . . and helped the elementary school kids win the Clarktown's Got Talent video contest."

"I'm not sure tripping and falling down qualifies as a routine," Max says.

I glare at him, but Kelli says brightly, "They totally

deserved to win!" She's just happy the high schoolers didn't win with their *Sound of Music* production.

Next year, I promise myself, the Clarktown's Got Talent video prize is going to the middle schoolers.

My inner scheming is interrupted by the next outtake coming on the screen.

It's of Auntie Li, Vivienne, and Mom giggling like teenagers as they watch Daniel practice his goose dance in full costume for the first time. The difference between Daniel's dancing and mine is that he's funny *on purpose*. Mom and her friends are practically falling onto each other for support, and Max isn't faring any better. He's laughing so hard that tears are streaming from his eyes even though he's been helping Daniel with the dance.

There are a bunch more outtakes.

Dad trying to make small talk with the Klingon while Stacey translates.

Tina and the other girls flipping their fans to the beat of Lizzo while Vivienne asks, "What in the world is that?" She looks directly into the camera. "Lily Hong, is this your doing?"

"Sorry!" The tablet picks up my guilty gulp. "I thought it could be fun. . . ."

The outtakes end there, and Tina laughs. "Vivienne nixed that idea right away."

"So are you going to be taking dance classes with Tina, Max, and Daniel after school?" Kelli asks me.

Tina already knows my answer, but she gives me a supportive smile before diving back into the gigantic sundae.

I shake my head and take a bite of the sundae. "No. The performance ended up being fun, but I don't think dancing is my thing. I've got other things I want to work on."

Lauren raises an eyebrow. "I know that look. You have another film idea, don't you?"

"Lots of film ideas, actually." Using my fingers, I snatch up the maraschino cherry Max was trying to get with his spoon.

"Hey, I wanted that!" he protests.

In bewilderment, Tina looks at the sundae, studded with cherries. "There are other cherries," she points out.

"This one is the best." I smile and eat it.

"Maybe I should take back my offer to let you use my video-editing studio," Max grumbles.

"But not until we finish filming *The Chosen One Slays Big Business: A Musical in Three Parts*, right?" Kelli asks anxiously.

It turns out that both Tina and Max can sing, and Lauren actually has a decent voice despite her hatred of musicals. She's agreed to be in it "just this once." Daniel is going to be involved too. He sings about as well as I do (so not well), but unlike me, he's game for anything. So now we have a cast again.

"Of course." I smile and wipe whipped cream off my chin. "But after that, I thought we could try something different." I stand up.

Kelli digs her spoon into the sundae. "Better eat up before the ice cream melts, everyone. This could take a while."

"Don't rush the creative process." I shoot her a mock-offended look and start pacing.

My mind races as I walk back and forth, ignoring the other customers staring at me. Not another musical. I'm not done with mythical/fairy-tale/supernatural films, but the community center documentary was cool too. I think about all those stories that we just started to tell. . . .

Finally, I come to a stop. Placing my hands on the pink Formica table, I lean forward and say, "I've got it!"

My friends put down their spoons.

"Is there a part for Theseus?" Max asks.

Uh, no. "Theseus is already the star of *Of Mice and Mazes*," I say tactfully, "so I think he's already had his moment."

"Good point," Max says reluctantly. "What's your idea, then?"

"Yeah, let's hear it, Lily!" Lauren says.

"I'm ready." Kelli rubs her stomach. "I can't eat another bite of ice cream anyway."

"This is so cool." Tina bounces in her seat.

"Okay, here it is." I close my eyes as a vision of our

future takes shape in my head. Opening my eyes again, I see my four best friends looking back at me with anticipation on their faces. This community I'm so lucky to be a part of.

I take a breath and announce my idea. "We're going to do a YouTube series about Clarktown!"

"Love it." Tina's eyes are shining. "Will the Chinese school be in it?"

"Of course. The community center too." Clarktown wouldn't be Clarktown without its heart.

"Ooh, maybe I could do some beauty tips like all those influencers. . . ." Kelli's eyes go dreamy as she trails off.

"The youth climate summit!" Lauren says. "That has to be in the series."

"The Fencing Team should be in it too," I add slyly. Since her knockout performance in the show, Lauren has become an official member of the Fencing Team.

She flushes. "Yeah, that would be good."

"And Theseus can—" Max begins.

"Max!" If he says another word about his rat . . .

"What?" He grins. "I was going to say Theseus can sit this out." *Do rats even sit?* "But I do have an idea for the series. I've only been in Clarktown for two years, but there's a lot I still don't understand. What's up with the clock tower being stuck at three thirty all the time? How can Mr. Cole make a living by selling only purple potatoes at the farmers market? Why did the city tell my parents that they couldn't build anything in the north-east corner lot in the Palisades?"

Okay. So . . . the answers to those questions are:

A. No one knows; we all just accept it.

B. Mr. Cole is able to make a living because everyone knows to buy at least a pound of purple potatoes from him every week (which is basically the same answer as A, now that I think of it).

C. What northeast corner lot in the Palisades?

I do my best to grin mysteriously. "Don't worry. Our series will reveal all."

"Then I have a question too," Tina says, and I remember that she doesn't live in Clarktown even though she goes to Chinese school at our community center. "Why is there a random picture of your mom at the Ice Yum Palace?"

"What are you talking about?" The picture she's pointing to is one that I must have seen a million times before. It's a fuzzy shot of a grinning teenager holding a gigantic golden trophy so that it half covers her face. "That's not my mom."

"Um, Lily?" Lauren is peering at the picture like she's seeing it for the first time. "I think it is."

Max nods. "Me too."

I look closer and my eyes widen as I recognize the jut of her chin and shape of her eyebrows. Holy wow. It *is* my mom. "That's weird. I guess she must have won the ice cream eating contest." I didn't think Mom was the type to enter a contest like that, but it's the only thing that makes sense. This is the Ice Yum Palace, after all, and Kelli's dad does hold an ice cream eating contest every year.

Kelli shakes her head. "If that's your mom as a teenager, then it was before Dad opened the Ice Yum Palace. I think this used to be a pub or maybe a restaurant."

Okay, I do actually remember my parents talking about how the ice cream parlor used to be something else. But if my mom didn't win an ice cream eating contest, then what's the trophy for?

"There's something written on the trophy," Max says, "but it's too small to read."

"On it." Pulse racing, I take a picture of the picture with my tablet. My friends gather around me as I zoom in on the writing. My breath stops when I see what it says.

Clarktown Roller Derby Queen.

Mom was the Roller Derby Queen?! Why am I finding out about this for the first time? You'd think Mom would have mentioned that she was a *freaking roller derby queen* when Vivienne asked about the old skating rink (okay, there was a lot going on that night, so I can see why it didn't come up). But I didn't even know our town had *had* a roller derby.

The others look as surprised as I am, but some other

feeling is starting to well up in me. I think it might be . . . excitement.

"Roller Derby Queen?" Max asks. "What does that even mean?"

"It means," I say, "that Clarktown has more secrets to discover."

We all grin at each other, and everyone scrambles to their feet. It's a good thing that the ice cream is pretty much gone because none of us can wait another minute to get started.

I pick up my tablet from the table. "Let's go. We have a YouTube series to film." All the possible stories, just waiting to be told, make my heart beat fast in anticipation. "This is going to be epic."

A NOTE FROM THE AUTHOR

DEAR READERS,

The legend "The Phoenix and Her City" is an important part of *The Unbeatable Lily Hong*, and I'd like to share some background about this story. I have always loved the story for its powerful themes of community, and it made sense for this mythical tale to be in my book about a myth-loving Chinese American girl desperate to save a community center, the heart of her own town.

But I also have a more personal reason for including this story from the Hui people, a Chinese Muslim minority group.

Like Lily, I am Hui. And like Lily, I have found that my stories end up taking forms different from what I had originally intended.

Fifteen years ago, I was trying to finish my first novel—a literary adult novel based on the myth of the phoenix who saves the city she loves by turning her body into its protection. To say that this book was a challenge would be an understatement (this was before I realized that I'm a children's book writer at heart), but I don't regret writing that first novel because it led me to the phoenix's city. And I mean that literally.

In a desperate attempt to finish my book, I saved up my money, took the summer off from teaching, and headed to Yinchuan, the capital city of the Ningxia Hui Autonomous Region in China.

Once I got there, everyone I met asked me why I was bypassing bigger, more "interesting" cities to visit their small city bordering the desert. I explained that I was writing a book that was partly set in Yinchuan. Of course, the question that followed was always: "What is your book about?"

Unfortunately, my rudimentary Chinese failed me when I tried to answer (and I'm not sure I could have explained it in English either).

Even though I had no clue as to what my book was about, I somehow managed to complete a first draft when I was in Yinchuan. And I also fell in love with the city on the edge of a desert. When the time finally came to leave and return to my life in the United States, it was hard to say goodbye. With many tears and hugs, I thanked everyone for their support and promised that I would finish my novel. My new Yinchuan friends said they couldn't wait to read it.

The Unbeatable Lily Hong isn't the book I promised them fifteen years ago in the sand-swept city of Yinchuan. But it's the book of my heart, and this time, I *can* explain what it's about.

It is a story about a girl who loves her town and its people.

Thank you for reading *The Unbeatable Lily Hong*, and I hope you enjoyed reading about Lily, her family, friends, one former archenemy, and the community of Clark-town!

Diana Ma

ACKNOWLEDGMENTS

MY HEART IS SO FULL of all the support and encouragement I got on this book! I have so many people to thank that I don't know where to start, but I will start with the incredible Angela Song, my first editor at Clarion Books. Angela, thank you so much for championing this book and for the fun chats about Chinese school—your editorial vision made this book what it is, and you were such a joy to work with! I also want to thank Alessandra Preziosi, my wonderful editor who saw *The Unbeatable Lily Hong* to the finish line! My warmest gratitude goes out to the entire Clarion Books team, especially Mary Wilcox, Ginny Bloom, and Margaret Crocker.

Always, always, always—I must thank Christa Heschke and Daniele Hunter, who are the best agents ever! Thank you also to Christina Scheuer, friend/collaborator/critique partner extraordinaire, for reading the initial chapter and giving invaluable feedback. Thank you to Melissa Grinley, not only for being my slayerette friend, but for great comments on the initial chapter. Thank you to We Need Diverse Books for the WNDB mentorship and Swati Avasthi for being my fantastic mentor.

I also want to thank the Highlights Foundation and the Doris Duke Foundation for Islamic Arts for creating and generously supporting and funding the Muslim Storytellers Fellowship. I can't even begin to express what this opportunity has meant to me. Zaynah Qutubuddan, Alison Green Myers, and George Brown from the Highlights Foundation have my unending gratitude for making this program possible and so, so much more. Zaynah, I screamed with joy in the parking lot when I got your voicemail saying I was accepted into the fellowship, and it's everything I could have possibly imagined! Thank you to Nafiza Azad and S. A. Chakraborty, my phenomenal mentors, and all the wonderful mentors in this program—S. K. Ali, Hatem Aly, Hena Khan, Sabaa Tahir, and Jamilah Thompkins-Bigelow. Thank you also to the incredible Narmeen Lakhani and M. O. Yuksel from the programming committee. You are all so welcoming and supportive (not to mention *brilliant*).

A huge thank-you goes out to all my fellow Muslim storytellers! This book is about community, and I am so grateful to this beautiful Muslim storytellers community for accepting and embracing me at a time when I desperately needed this. The sense of belonging that the residents of Clarktown find in their community center is what I got from all of you. Lily, my main character in the book, didn't start out as Muslim, but once I brought in the phoenix myth, a story from the Hui people, I knew Lily needed to be Hui (Chinese Muslim) like me. And I'm not sure if I would have been able to draw from my own culture and identity to write Lily's story if it hadn't been for this community, so again, thank you!

Specifically, thank you to my insightful, compassionate, and *hilarious* peer workshop group of Intisar Khanani, Heba Helmy, Loretta Chefchaouni, and Fatima Samatar. I love our peer workshops so much, and I am so lucky to be in your company! Thank you also to Huda Al-Murashi for helpful chats about writing Muslim characters in middle grade books at one of our retreats. I had so many great conversations with so many of you, but I'm afraid that if I start trying to list them all, I'm going to accidentally leave some out. I'll stop here, but please know that I treasure every interaction I've had with you!

Thank you to Joel, my husband, for his unerring support; Kieran, my youngest kid, for his faith in me (I'm his third-favorite author—yay!); and Liam, my eldest kid, for serving as my somewhat reluctant in-house twelve-year-old resource. Thank you to my parents for making me go to Chinese school and to my brother, David, for letting me use the pennies he never needed. Thank you to my Chinese dance teacher for putting up with my dropped fans and for making me the lead dancer solely because of my height (no, I'm not that tall, and yes, I basically stopped growing any taller after the age of twelve). Thank you to the people of Yinchuan, the city of the phoenix in the myth that is so central to Lily's story. And finally, thank you to YOU, my readers!

ABOUT THE AUTHOR

DIANA MA is a Chinese American author who writes young adult and middle grade books that feature Asian American heroes. She believes that it's important for all kids to recognize themselves as the heroes of the books they read. Her belief that diverse books help us create a better world is what drives her writing. She has two wonderful kids of her own and wants them to grow up with books that represent them. Diana was a 2019 We Need Diverse Books mentee with Swati Avasthi and a 2021 Highlights Foundation Muslim Storytellers Fellow. She also teaches at a community college in Seattle. Visit her at dianamaauthor.com.